HELD BY YOU

RIDING TALL

CHEYENNE MCCRAY

CHAPTER 1

*S*ee you, Ricki," Hollie Simmons called out to the owner of Sweet Things Bakery. Hollie juggled two large pink boxes of holiday cookies as she pressed her hip against the glass door of the bakery. "Merry Christmas."

Ricki gave a little wave. "Bye, Hollie. Hope those kiddos of yours enjoy the goodies."

Before Hollie could push the door open with her hip, it swung wide, catching Hollie off guard. She stumbled out of the bakery and gave a little cry, knowing in that instant that she and her cookies were going to land hard and scatter across the sidewalk.

A man's strong arm caught her around her shoulders, dragging her up against a hard chest. At the same time her savior caught her, he caught the cookies in his opposite hand, gracefully saving them from their fate of moments before.

"Oh! Thank you." Hollie let out a breath of relief as the unseen man steadied her. The bakery door closed, leaving her on the sidewalk with the man who still held her. She caught a sexy masculine scent that was warm despite the December chill in the air. She tried to turn but he didn't immediately set her free, ensuring she was steady on her feet.

He dropped his arm from around her shoulders but kept his hold on the cookies. She turned and hitched her purse up on her shoulder. It was Lieutenant John McBride who had just saved her from a nasty fall.

"Lieutenant McBride." For no reason whatsoever, her stomach gave a little flip. Okay, maybe there was a reason...and that reason was wrapped up in a six-foot-two, brown-eyed, dark-haired package wearing a uniform fitted to perfection on a powerfully muscled body. "Thanks so much."

"It was my fault." He shook his head. "I didn't see you and I opened the door at the same time you were coming out."

"Whatever the case, thanks for catching me." She smiled. "Protect and serve. You're doing a great job of it."

He gave a little grin that surprised her. She didn't know the police lieutenant personally, but whenever she had seen him, he had never been wearing a smile. He always seemed so serious. That hadn't stopped her from having a little crush on him from afar. She'd always found the man incredibly attractive from a distance. His seriousness, his hard expression, had made her want to know more about the man and what made him tick.

She'd always been too shy to go up to him and introduce herself when she'd seen him around town. With her full curves, and stepbrothers who had belittled her constantly since she was a child, her confidence wasn't the best.

Lieutenant McBride raised the boxes of cookies. "Let me take these to your car."

"Thanks." She nodded toward her small Honda parked along the curb.

He walked at her side as she headed for the car. "Are these for your students?" His question surprised her and she cut her gaze to his. "I imagine today you're having holiday parties at the elementary school."

She blinked. "You know who I am?"

2

He gave a slow grin. "How could I not know one of the best kindergarten teachers in the school district, Ms. Simmons? You have an excellent reputation."

"I could say the same about you." She couldn't help but smile again as they reached the car's driver's side door, which she unlocked with the remote. "But it is nice to actually meet you in person."

He gave a nod and opened the car door for her with one hand, still holding the cookie boxes with his other. Before she could extend her hands to take the boxes from him, he leaned past her, into her car, and set the cookies on the passenger seat.

When he drew back, his body brushed hers. She felt a shiver run through her that had absolutely nothing to do with the cold, and she swallowed as her body reacted to his nearness. She wanted her few moments with John McBride to last. She wasn't ready to part company with him yet...and she wanted to see him again. Now how could she possibly arrange that?

A thought came to her and she cleared her throat. "After the holidays, I'm having a career day in my class. Do you think you might have time in your schedule to visit my children?"

John studied her in a way that made her stomach flip. She found herself holding her breath as if she'd just asked him out on a date.

He gave a slow nod. "I'd enjoy that."

She let out her breath in a rush. "So would I—I mean the children."

Again a sexy little smile. "Why don't I call you and we'll set up a date and time?"

"Sure." She tried to compose herself after her slip up and clasped the strap of her purse for something to do with her hands as he pulled a small spiral-bound notebook from his shirt pocket. "Going to put me in there with all of your suspects and criminals?"

This time he gave a low laugh. "I have a section reserved just for you."

A flutter went through her midsection again. Was he flirting with her? Yes, he was definitely flirting with her.

She gave him her number and he jotted it down before tucking the notepad into his uniform pocket again. He pulled out a business card with a police shield, Prescott Police Department, and his name and number on it. She held onto the card as she looked up at him.

"You have a good day, Ms. Simmons," he said.

"Please call me Hollie," she said. "I hope your day is great too."

He gave a nod. "Hollie." The way he said her name about made her melt. His voice was warm and deep and at that moment had a caress to it. She had no doubt that his tone would turn hard in a flash when necessary.

It didn't surprise her that he didn't tell her to call him by his first name. After all, she didn't know him well and he was an officer of the law and had to maintain a certain amount of distance in public.

She gave him one last smile before climbing into her car. She dropped his business card into her purse as he closed the door behind her.

After she turned on her car, he watched her back out of her parking space. His presence made her so nervous she almost backed into a passing car and she had to jam her foot on the brake pedal. Her face flushed with heat and she did her best not to look at John McBride as she guided her vehicle out of the spot and headed toward the elementary school.

John had to hold back a smile as he watched a flustered Hollie Simmons drive away. No doubt she was embarrassed because she'd almost hit another vehicle with hers while a police officer looked on. Maybe he shouldn't want to smile, but she was so damned cute he couldn't help it. And now he had her phone number in his pocket.

The pretty elementary school teacher had such innocent honey-gold eyes, a soft smile, and soft, generous curves. He'd noticed her several times at various local functions but had never approached her. A twinge of disappointment went through him that he couldn't have spent a little more time talking with her by her car.

It was hard to believe Hollie Simmons was related in any way to the trouble-making redneck brothers, Carl, Dickey, and Floyd Whitfield. But then again, she was their stepsister and wasn't blood-related. Still, he couldn't imagine her growing up with three men who were at complete odds with her sweet disposition.

He headed toward his sister-in-law's bakery. It was Friday and his turn to pick up donuts for the station. As he walked, he continued to think about Hollie and frowned. What had happened to his decision to never date any woman from Prescott, much less flirt with anyone?

As a matter of fact, he didn't "date" anyone. He had casual relationships with women he'd met in Flagstaff and Sedona. Nadia, who lived in Sedona, was one of those women, and she had become a friend with benefits. Theirs was a relationship based on the understanding that either one of them could walk away and they would remain friends with no regrets. It was a satisfactory arrangement that had carried on over the past six months.

He didn't think there was the right woman out there for him. Until he reached a point where he would leave his chosen career, he was married to his job and no woman wanted a man whose loyalties were to his badge first. He'd seen a lot of cop marriages fail, and he didn't intend to become one of the sad statistics.

Maybe one day, when he was ready to move on, then he would consider a relationship.

John glanced at the large plate glass window that was frosted around the edges as if snow was on it and had *Happy Holidays* written in an arch over a winter scene. He grabbed the cold door handle, pulling the bakery door open, and walking inside. Warm smells of baked bread and pastries flowed over him and chased away the cold. Ricki smiled at him from behind a pastry case.

"'Morning, John." Ricki gave him a winning smile as she brought out pink boxes that would fit a dozen donuts each. His sister-in-law was a pretty woman with blonde hair and hazel eyes. "Two dozen?"

"You've got it." John dug in his pocket for his wallet and slipped out enough cash to pay for the donuts as she set the pastry boxes on the donut display case. "How's your day starting out?"

"Great." She opened the case, grabbed a small piece of wax paper, and used it to pick up donuts as she began putting an assortment into the pink boxes. She put an extra Long John in the box as usual since she knew it was his favorite type of donut. His stepmother had always made them when he was a kid.

Just as he finished paying for the donuts, his radio squawked. The dispatcher asked for units to respond to the report of a body found on the south side of town. John answered the dispatcher, indicating that he was on his way. He carried the boxes of donuts toward the door as he said goodbye to Ricki over his shoulder before hurrying out of the bakery at a brisk pace.

So much for taking donuts to the station while they were still warm and fresh.

Today John was on his own. Yesterday on a call, a Rottweiler had come out of nowhere and had taken a chunk out of Jamie Cruz's leg and the young officer had been forced to take a few days off. Having recently moved to Prescott, Jamie was John's new partner and John hadn't had much of an opportunity to get to know the officer. From what John had seen, dog bite notwithstanding, Jamie seemed to be a good, more than competent cop.

John tossed the donut boxes onto the passenger seat as he climbed into his cruiser. It had been two minutes at most from the time the call had come in to the moment John was in the car and headed to the south side of town.

CHAPTER 2

*I*t didn't take long for John to reach the address where a small crowd had gathered. Another cruiser arrived at the same time John did and both vehicles parked in front of the apartment building and the crowd. Officers Pablo Suarez and Darryl Taylor climbed out of their cruiser as John left his.

Immediately, Suarez and Taylor began securing the scene while John went to the body that he could see, now that Taylor had ordered the crowd to back away. John crouched beside the man's corpse.

The body lay on the sidewalk, his face—what was left of it—turned to the side. Blood was congealing on the cold concrete.

Anger burned through John at the thought of all the violence and murder that had been occurring in Prescott. Dark days had come to the town that had been quiet before the drug trade and even human trafficking had reared its ugly head. He felt a disillusionment with his home town. As a cop he could fight to clean up the trash in the town, but he resented the fact that so much had invaded the once peaceful town.

"Shotgun to the face." Suarez crouched beside John and

gestured to the tattoo on the man's neck. "Jesus Perez's gang. Who do you think the victim is this time?"

"Hard to tell." John frowned as he saw a bulge in the victim's back pocket. "Maybe this will clue us in."

John pulled on a latex glove and tugged the worn leather wallet out of the pocket. He flipped it open. "Looks like someone took care of our latest problem." He held out the driver's license.

"Rudy Garcia." Suarez whistled through his teeth. "Merry Christmas."

"If this is Rudy, Jesus' gang is short another top man." John nodded. "This smells of Freddy Victors. He was likely getting revenge for the death of his own man, Hurley Cartwright."

Suarez nodded. "We haven't been able to prove that Jesus killed Hurley, or that Freddy killed Jesus' brother, Juan, but we will." John swept his gaze over the body in front of him. "Sooner rather than later."

"This is getting nasty," Suarez said.

John frowned. "Ever since Johnny Rocha was taken down and killed, the two gangs trying to take over his territory are getting bolder and bolder. If you can call Freddy and his redneck lackeys a gang."

With a mirthless smile, Suarez said, "Maybe they'll solve the problem by taking each other out until none of the bastards are left."

John got to his feet, looked over his shoulder, and saw his stepbrother, Reese McBride, who was a detective with the Prescott Police Department. "Reese and Carter are here." John watched his stepbrother who walked beside his new partner, Detective Will Carter.

Reese had light brown hair, square features, and was as tall as John. His stepbrother was missing two fingers from his left hand from an explosion a few months back. He'd recently married his former partner, Detective Kelley Petrova.

Carter, whose skin was a dark shade of rich mahogany, was two inches taller than Reese's six-two. He was built like a runner and from what John had heard, the man was as fast as he looked, maybe even faster than Reese, who had always been an exceptional sprinter.

When Reese and Carter stopped beside John and Suarez, John gave the newcomers a nod each. He held up the wallet. "Rudy Garcia, who appears to have taken it in the face with a shotgun."

Carter narrowed his gaze. "Just like Juan Perez."

"If we don't get this under control," Reese said with a frown, "we're going to end up with a real problem."

Carter nodded. "You've got that right."

In moments, John and the other officers were combing the area for clues. Reese and Carter spoke with bystanders, trying to find a witness to the murder. When the medical examiner examined the body, he confirmed that the man had been murdered shortly before the police reached the scene.

As they worked the scene, John's thoughts turned to Hollie, the sweet stepsister of the men who were at the top of the department's list of suspects for the deaths of Rudy Garcia and Jesus Perez's brother, Juan. John wondered if Hollie could be in danger just by being around her stepbrothers. Jesus could possibly target Hollie to get back at the Whitfield brothers. Not that the brothers probably cared.

The thought made anger rise in John's chest, burning with a ferocity that surprised him, yet didn't. He felt an unusually strong need to protect Hollie. It was more than simply the desire to watch over the innocent…it was the need to protect someone he cared about. It didn't make a hell of a lot of sense because he barely knew Hollie, and today was the first time he'd ever spoken with her. But there it was.

A spot of red, almost hidden in a clump of dry yellow grass, caught John's eye and he walked toward it. With some satisfaction, he saw that it was a shotgun shell. He pulled out a clear plastic evidence bag and used his gloved hand to pick up the shell and drop it into the bag.

"Reese." John held up the evidence. "If we're lucky, we'll get prints off the shell."

"Good." Reese gave a nod. "Looks like that's our only evidence so far. Doesn't seem that we have any witnesses. At least none who will admit they saw anything."

"This shell also gives us a reason to pick up Freddy Victors for questioning." John handed the evidence bag to Reese. "He carries a shotgun in the gun racks in his truck."

"Since Cruz is out, you need backup," Reese said. "Carter and I will head to Freddy's with you."

John strode toward his cruiser and climbed in while Reese and his partner went to their unmarked vehicle. As he drove, John mulled the crime over in his mind. Every now and then his thoughts would touch on Hollie, distracting him and causing him to frown. He shook his head as he turned into the trailer park where Freddy lived. It wasn't like him to get distracted by anything, especially by a woman.

But Hollie wasn't just any woman.

He blew out his breath as he reached the trailer and a beat-up old Ford club cab truck parked out front that belonged to Carl Whitfield, one of Hollie's stepbrothers. Freddy Victors' newer truck was next to it.

Freddy was sitting on the porch with Carl. Both Freddy and Carl were sitting on shabby lawn chairs beneath the mobile home's tattered and faded green awning. They wore jackets, ball caps, and work boots. Carl had his hands stuffed into the pockets of his jacket, presumably to keep them warm. John didn't plan to take any chances that Carl wasn't keeping a weapon in his jacket pocket.

John parked and shut off the engine before climbing out of

the vehicle, his gaze remaining focused on the two rednecks. Reese and Carter pulled up in their car, parked, and got out of their vehicles, too. John had already started toward the men, the detectives following him.

Freddy had always been a cocky sonofabitch with a permanent sneer on his average face. He had straight light-brown hair that was barely visible with the John Deere cap on his head. His eyes were muddy brown, his skin littered with pockmarks from having had chicken pox as an adult.

Carl, on the other hand, was considered the pretty boy of the brothers, which wasn't saying much. Blond-haired and blue-eyed, Carl had a darkness in his gaze that reflected something sick inside of him.

Disgust for the Whitfield brothers and Freddy Victors was something John had to work hard at holding back. From the time they were kids, Freddy and the Whitfields had been bullies and nothing but trouble. As pre-teens they'd been accused of stealing bikes, toys, and other items. They'd also been suspected of mutilating and killing small animals but had never been caught in the act.

When they were teenagers, Freddy and the Whitfields had been arrested for underage drinking and for possession of illegal substances. They'd broken into homes, stealing whatever they could. Eventually they'd been arrested, tried, and convicted as juveniles for the thefts, and sent to the juvenile detention center more than once. Of course those records were sealed, but John was the same age as the oldest Whitfield brother, Floyd, and knew firsthand how rotten the brothers were.

As adults the Whitfield brothers had been arrested for disturbing the peace, carrying a gun without a permit, and had done some time for narcotics possession.

Unlike the Whitfields, somehow Freddy had avoided getting caught and prosecuted for the same acts, which was how he managed to get a gun permit. John knew with everything he had that Freddy had been just as guilty as the Whitfields in their past misdeeds, but Freddy had never been convicted.

John ground his teeth as he approached the two men sitting outside the trailer. He couldn't stand men like the Whitfields and Freddy. One of these days, if they were indeed guilty of murder, the men would land in the penitentiary. John would see to it.

He reached the men as Freddy gave a broad grin. "Hi, Officer. What brings you around here?"

John would have liked to punch the grin right off of Freddy's face, but schooled his expression. "Where have you been this morning?"

"Right here with good ol' Carl." The grin didn't leave Freddy's face. "We haven't left the place. So what's the problem, Officer?"

"Your neighbors can corroborate that you've been sitting in front of your trailer all morning?" John asked.

Freddy shrugged. "We were inside a while."

John walked to the closest truck, Victor's newer white Ford, which had a rifle and a shotgun in the gun racks in the window of the cab. John set his palm on the hood that was warm to the touch despite the December chill in the air. He focused his gaze on Carl, who appeared to be having a harder time than Freddy looking at ease.

"Someone's been driving this truck." John removed his hand from the surface. "Want to try telling me your story again?"

A flash of something crossed Freddy's face but his smile broadened. "Carl here ran to that mart on the corner."

"You said both of you haven't left the place," John said. "You're changing your story?"

Freddy kept grinning. "It was only a quick run."

John turned his gaze on Carl. "What did you buy?"

Uncertainty glinted in Carl's gaze. "Uh—"

"A six-pack." Freddy inclined his head toward the trailer. "It's in the fridge."

"I didn't ask you." John gave Freddy a hard look before he turned his gaze back on Carl. "What did you buy, Carl?"

"Like Freddy said." Carl shifted in his seat. "Beer."

"We'll have the surveillance videos checked." John watched both Carl and Freddy and neither seemed concerned. Likely they knew that the little mart didn't have surveillance cameras. They'd been shot out not long ago and the owners of the mart hadn't had the money to have them replaced.

John had already seen Freddy's gun permit when he'd been questioned about Juan Perez's murder, so he didn't ask to see it again.

"We're going to need you to come down to the station." Reese nodded toward John's cruiser. "We have more questions for you."

Freddy's smirk stayed. "You haven't said what this is about, stubby," he said, clearly referring to Reese's hand.

"That's Detective McBride to you," Carter said, his deep voice holding a hint of danger.

John managed not to growl and instead hardened his gaze.

Reese didn't appear to have noticed or cared about the slight in regards to his missing fingers. "We'll tell you all about it at the station."

Freddy and Carl didn't move. "You've got no reason to take us in."

"You're coming with us, in handcuffs or not, it doesn't matter," John said. "You decide."

"Whatever you want." Freddy pushed himself up from his porch seat, Carl following his lead. John gave a nod toward his cruiser and the pair headed toward it.

As a precaution, Freddy and Carl were both patted down. Both had pocketknives, which John confiscated for the time being, but no other weapons. The entire time, Freddy made wiseass remarks.

John ground his teeth and said nothing as he opened the back door to the cruiser and the men scooted inside. John shut the door firmly behind them before climbing into the front seat. He backed up the vehicle and during the short distance to the station he ignored Freddy's questions as to why they were being taken in.

Once they were inside the station, Freddy and Carl were placed in separate interview rooms. John watched through the one-way glass as Reese and Carter interviewed Freddy. The man maintained that he'd been at his trailer and didn't know anything about the murder of Rudy Garcia. The whole time Freddy acted like it was a big joke. It was probably a good thing that it was Reese and Carter doing the interviewing because John wanted to knock the shit eating grin right off Freddy's face.

The interview with Carl Whitfield went similarly to Freddy's. Carl was clearly nervous about something, but kept to the same story as Freddy had. John was surprised at Carl's nervousness this time around. Usually he was unshakeable, but this time something was different. Something had changed in the dynamic between Freddy and Carl.

At the end of each interview, Reese told the men, individually, that they would remain at the station for further questioning. Freddy had scowled, the first crack in the mask of amusement he'd been wearing ever since John had driven up to the man's trailer.

John watched as the men were taken away to separate holding cells. Reese and Carter walked into the observation room.

"What do you think?" Reese asked John.

John shook his head. "They're full of shit and Freddy is a good actor but he was definitely hiding something. Carl looked close to cracking."

Reese nodded. "Maybe a little more time in the holding cell will convince him to talk."

"He's been in that position too many times over the years,"

John said. "Frankly, I'm not sure it's going to matter. We need to get something on them and get it now."

Reese nodded as he folded his arms across his chest. "Damn it. Whatever it takes. We *will not* let these sonofabitches get away with murder."

CHAPTER 3

*H*ollie finished doling out the holiday cookies in star, bell, tree, stocking, and wreath shapes. The cookies were frosted with red and green icing along with red, green, and white sprinkles. She had two Jewish students to whom she gave blue and white cookies decorated with menorahs.

"Thank you, Miss Simmons," the students chimed as they were each given a cookie.

She smiled, as the kindergarteners bit into the most delicious sugar cookies Hollie had ever tasted. Ricki's bakery was one of the best things that had happened to Prescott as far as Hollie was concerned. She sighed and resisted patting her belly. It was true that she enjoyed sweets a little too much.

Thoughts of her stepbrothers' remarks about her generous figure made her stomach clench. Every time she was around Floyd, Dickey, and Carl, they made comments about her appearance and were cruel in their remarks. They were the only family she had, but truth be told, she wouldn't have minded never seeing them again.

Unfortunately, they lived with her on the ranch she'd inherited from her father. She'd been named her father's sole heir. In the will, her three stepbrothers had received sums of fifty thousand dollars each, which they promptly squandered away somehow. She didn't really want to know what they did with their money.

They made constant jibes about her being the favorite and that she should split the ranch with them. Hollie had steadfastly refused—it had been the one thing she'd been able to remain strong about. The ranch had been in the Simmons family for generations and she wasn't going to let her stepbrothers ruin it and sell it off. It was the only time she'd been able to say no to her stepbrothers.

It wasn't a working ranch anymore, but she hoped that one day it would be again.

And then there was their friend, Freddy, who was always around. He made frequent sexual remarks to her, and just thinking about them made her shudder.

She pushed thoughts of Freddy aside. Why ruin a perfectly good day?

As the kids ate their cookies, she thought about her mother and felt an ache in her chest. Her mother, Marilyn, had been a southern belle who had taught Hollie to be gentle and loving, and somewhat prim and proper. Hollie knew that her mother had been her father's only true love. It was two years after Marilyn had been killed in a car accident that Hollie's father, Joe Simmons, had married Betty Whitfield. He seemed to have been under the impression that Hollie needed a mother figure around.

Hollie would have been better off without a female influence when it came to having Betty Whitfield as a stepmother and her three sons as stepbrothers. Hollie had grown up feeling something like Cinderella but with three stepbrothers rather than stepsisters. She was still waiting for her fairy godmother, crystal slippers, and prince.

Inwardly Hollie sighed. When her father had been killed in a freak accident, she'd felt like her whole world was crumbling.

Betty had become more and more vicious in her attacks on Hollie, and she'd had nowhere to escape.

A chain smoker, Betty had died from lung cancer. Her passing had been a relief to Hollie, if she was honest with herself. And she was almost always honest with herself. She felt some shame for feeling that way about a human life, even one as despicable as Betty, but she couldn't help it.

The feeling of being set free came to a resounding halt when Hollie's brothers took over where their mother had left off. They'd thought they would inherit the ranch, not knowing that Betty had signed a prenuptial agreement that left the ranch to Hollie.

Hollie stood straighter. None of that mattered now. The important things in her life were her job and her students, who were like her own children.

In her jeans' pocket her phone vibrated, but she ignored it. She never answered her phone until school was out.

She glanced at the clock to see that the school day was almost over and turned her attention to the students. "Time to get your things together. Don't forget the Christmas cards and gifts you made for your families. When you're ready, line up at the door."

The room was filled with scuffling noises and chatter as the students pulled on jackets and gathered their things. Soon they were lined up, ready for Hollie to walk them to the buses and parent pickup.

She led them down the hallway that was decorated with red and green handmade decorations for the holidays. As they walked outside, a chilly breeze made Hollie break out in goose bumps beneath her light blue holiday sweater with its big snowman wearing a Santa hat. At the end of the hat was a fluffy white ball along with smaller green balls for buttons on the snowman's chest. The sweater wasn't enough against the chill and she rubbed her arms, regretting having forgotten to wear her own jacket.

As her students met with their parents or climbed into school buses, they waved at Hollie and called out with farewells of "Merry Christmas" and "Happy Holidays." She waved in return and smiled at the children.

When the kids were safely taken care of, Hollie shivered as she walked back to her classroom. Her phone vibrated again and she pulled it out of her pocket and checked the caller ID. Her stomach dropped as she recognized the number that had appeared on the phone's screen too many times in the past. It was the number of the police department. Likely one of her stepbrothers was in trouble again and needed her to pick him up or bail him out. She prayed it wasn't to bail one of them out. They were going through her savings way too often.

She considered ignoring the call, but a spark of hope went through her that maybe it was John McBride and not her brothers. She answered the phone with a hopeful, "Hello?"

"Why didn't you answer before?" came Carl's surly voice and Hollie's stomach dropped. "Need you to pick me and Freddy up at the police station."

Not Freddy. She couldn't stand Freddy and his lewd comments and the way he looked at her. She hated his influence on her stepbrothers. They were bad enough without Freddy around.

She bit her lip. She wanted to say an emphatic "NO" to Carl and tell him to find another ride. "Why can't Floyd or Dickey pick you up?" she said.

"They're busy." A sneer was in Carl's voice.

She walked from the cold outdoors into the warm building where her classroom was. "I've got things to do, Carl." She did her best to sound firm.

"I need you to pick up me and Freddy," Carl said in a nasty tone. "Hurry and get your fat ass down here or you'll regret it." He disconnected the call.

She slowly lowered the phone, her face hot, the backs of her eyes prickling. Truth was, she was afraid of her stepbrothers. She couldn't trust them and she was afraid they might hurt her or somehow get her involved in whatever terrible things they might be up to. They'd made threats in the past and she didn't trust them at all. She wasn't sure what they were capable of.

Heart thumping, face still burning, she shoved the phone into her pocket and walked into her classroom. She slipped on her coat and gathered her purse, as well as other things she needed to take home. She shut off the light and walked out into the hallway, and locked the classroom door behind her.

The entire drive to the police station, she cursed herself for her fear of her stepbrothers. She didn't know what would happen if she stood up to them again. The times she had stood up to them in the past, her cat mysteriously disappeared, all of her dishes had been broken, and one of her tires had been slashed, among other things.

The worst incident as an adult was when Floyd had shaken her so hard her neck hurt, her head ached, and he'd left bruises on her upper arms. He'd been livid at the time and she'd been terrified, more than anytime before. From the gleam of hatred in his eyes, she'd been so sure he had been about to strike her. Instead, he'd shoved her away from him and she would have fallen if a wall hadn't been behind her. Her head had struck the wall, hard, and she'd seen stars.

As she drove, she chewed one of her nails, a habit she'd acquired since Floyd, Carl, and Dickey had been brought into the family. The faces they'd shown her father had been so different than the way they were in reality.

When she arrived at the police station, she parked, got out and locked the doors, and headed inside. She prayed she wouldn't see John McBride. She wasn't sure she could take the embarrassment.

Freddy and Carl were waiting when she walked inside. Both men scowled at her.

"Why the fuck did you take so long?" Carl said.

"I got here as fast as I could." She hated how small her voice sounded and how she felt she had to defend herself.

Freddy jerked his head toward the front doors. "Let's get out of here."

Before they could take a step, John McBride walked through the station's entrance. Hollie's chest hurt at the hard look on his features as he took in Freddy, Carl, and her.

"Hi, Officer," Freddy said with a broad grin.

Lieutenant McBride's brows narrowed, but he passed them without saying a word.

Hollie's spirits sank even further. Was it just this morning that he'd saved her from a fall and had given her a smile?

Feeling a lot like Cinderella must have, Hollie followed Carl and Freddy outside. When she unlocked the car, Carl snatched the keys from her. "Get in the backseat, fat ass."

A flash of anger caused Hollie to grit her teeth but she opened up the rear passenger door, slid onto the seat, and buckled herself in. She had expected Carl to take the keys because they never let her drive. She hated the way every one of her stepbrothers drove, not to mention Freddy, one of the many reasons why she didn't like to pick them up. The way they sped and swerved every-where, they were bound to get someone killed and she didn't want to be a victim of their recklessness.

Carl drove to Freddy's trailer on the south side of town where their trucks were parked. Hollie let out a breath of relief that they'd made it and soon she could part company with them and be on her way.

She scooped her purse up off of the floorboard then climbed out of the car. Freddy and Carl stood near the driver's side door.

"Excuse me," she said, reaching for the door handle.

"Not so fast." Freddy slung his arm around her shoulders and brought her up close to him. His breath was hot as he spoke in her ear. "Stay and I'll show you what a real man is like."

"What, you have one in there?" she said before she could stop herself.

Freddy scowled and shoved her up against the car, his arm across her throat. "You better watch it, bitch. You understand me?"

Hollie swallowed, her throat hurting from the pressure of his arm. She said nothing as she tried not to look away from Freddy's muddy brown eyes.

He pressed his arm tighter and her eyes watered. "I said, do you understand, bitch?"

She could do nothing but whisper, "Yes."

Freddy pushed away from her. For a moment she thought he was going to hit her, but he just smirked. He and Carl bumped fists before Freddy headed for his front door.

Carl rounded on Hollie as she slid into the front seat of her Honda. "Get home and fix dinner, woman. I'm hungry."

Hollie snapped. All of the fury she felt for her stepbrothers and Freddy crashed down on her. "Fix your own dinner," she said before slamming her car door shut and putting the vehicle into gear. She refused to look at him as the car's tires spun before it lurched forward and she was driving away from where he stood. Against her will she glanced in the rearview mirror, saw the dark scowl on Carl's face, and shivered.

She chewed on her nails as she drove aimlessly for a while, not wanting to go home. As much as she loved Prescott, she sometimes wished she could leave this town and start somewhere new. Somewhere away from her brothers and their low-life friends, like Freddy Victors.

Dear God, she needed the strength to stand up to her step-brothers. Somehow she had to get them to stop bullying and threatening her, and scaring her. But how?

She'd never told anyone what happened at home, too embarrassed over her own inability to stand up to them and because of who and what her stepbrothers and their friends were. A bunch of no-good troublemakers.

Her breath left her in a rush. The longer she stayed away from home, the harder it was going to be to face them when she got there. If she didn't have to go home, she wouldn't.

To hell with Carl, Dickey, Floyd, and their friends, she thought, veering from the politeness of her mother's lessons on how to be a lady. Ladies didn't say things like "to hell with".

Right now she didn't give a damn about being a lady.

Who said she had to go home now? She gripped the steering wheel in one hand as she reached into her pocket for her cell phone. It might be a small act of defiance, but it felt good to make the decision to stay in town, at least for a little while.

CHAPTER 4

*M*usic poured out of the open doors of the Highlander, the beat pounding through Hollie's blood as she headed toward the bar. Her friend, Leigh Monroe, should be waiting for her and saving a table.

Hollie clutched her small purse and shivered from the chill in the air. She snuggled more deeply in her jacket as she walked. She didn't mind the cold—it was an excuse to wear sweaters and jackets. Although she might have chosen something other than a sweater with a big snowman and fuzzy balls on it to wear for a night out if she'd been able to go home without dealing with her stepbrothers.

The Highlander was decorated with red chili lights around the windows and colorful mini lights along the eaves.

When she entered the bar, smells of bar food and beer mixed with smoke. The odors flowed over her along with the bar's warm air. To her left was the dance floor that was filled with people doing the two-step, and beyond that were two pool tables and a dartboard. Even over the music she could hear the crack of billiards.

She looked to the right where the mechanical bull was in full swing. Up ahead she saw Leigh Monroe, a willowy blonde sitting at a table along with a petite woman who Hollie recognized as Detective Kelley Petrova-McBride. Next to her was Leigh's friend who was originally from Indiana, the redheaded Carilyn Thompson-McBride.

Lord, does everyone marry McBrides around here? Hollie thought to herself with amusement, then thought of John McBride and bit her lower lip. She likely didn't have a chance with him, but she could fantasize, couldn't she?

When she reached the three women, Leigh got up and hugged Hollie. "So glad you could make it," Leigh said, talking close enough to her ear that Hollie could hear her over the music. Leigh drew away and smiled, but something about her smile looked sad.

"What's wrong?" Hollie frowned.

"You're either extremely perceptive or I'm not very good at hiding things from you." Leigh's smile faltered. "Mike and I broke up."

"I'm sorry." Hollie squeezed her friend's hands. "Are you all right?"

Leigh smiled again. "I'm fine. Tonight is about having fun and not thinking about things that are a bummer, right?"

"You bet," Hollie gave Leigh an encouraging smile. It was obvious Leigh didn't want to talk about her breakup with Mike, at least not now. Frankly, Hollie didn't want to talk about things that were a bummer in her own life, namely her stepbrothers.

Leigh slid into her chair while Hollie set her small purse on the table then shrugged off her jacket. She put her jacket on the back of the chair next to Leslie's and greeted Kelley and Carilyn as she sat.

The four women had to talk over the loud music, but soon they had drinks and were laughing and chatting. Even Leigh looked happier than she had when Hollie had first walked in. There was still an edge of sadness to Leigh, but Hollie thought she was feeling a little better for the time being.

Hollie sipped on her rum and coke and found herself feeling warm inside and nice and tipsy. It was easy to push thoughts of her stepbrothers to the back of her mind. She'd really needed a drink to relax her after her time with Carl and Freddy, and she was celebrating the end of the semester and the upcoming holidays.

Kelley was telling a story about her new partner that made all the girls giggle, including Hollie, but her laughter died away when she felt a prickling at the nape of her neck. For one moment she was afraid one of her stepbrothers was behind her, but when she turned to glance over her shoulder, she was grateful she didn't see any of them.

What she did find was John McBride—and he was looking right at her.

Heat traveled through her from head to toe when he smiled at her. She returned his smile as the warmth pooled in her belly where she felt butterflies take flight.

His muscular body was clad in a black western shirt along with snug Wranglers, black boots, and a black Stetson. He was supposed to be the good guy in uniform, but he sure pulled off the bad boy look in his black hat.

He looked so sexy that she felt the flutter rise from her belly to her chest. He was a hard man, she knew that, but at that moment his edges seemed a little less rough, his demeanor a little softer than normal.

She thought her heart would stop when he walked toward her table. All noise seemed to vanish and all she could think about was the man who was coming closer and closer.

When he reached the table, he held her gaze. "How are you tonight, Teacher?"

She smiled at his teasing tone. "Quite well, thank you. And how are you, Lieutenant?"

"Getting better by the minute." His smile was warm and sexy and she felt another thrill run through her. He turned his gaze to her friends. "Hello, ladies."

Kelley gave him a quick grin. "Since when did you become such a gentleman, John?" She worked with him at the Prescott Police Department, so Hollie figured it was natural for Kelley to call John by his first name.

"I have my moments." He nodded to Leigh and Carilyn who greeted him in turn.

"Why don't you pull up a chair and join us?" Leigh propped her arms on the table. "We can make room."

John shook his head. "I stopped by to ask Hollie to dance."

Hollie's throat went dry and she felt a little shiver of pleasure. "I'd love to."

"We'll watch your stuff," Leigh said and gestured toward Hollie's purse.

"Thank you." Hollie cleared her throat and turned her attention back to John.

He held out his hand and she took it. His hand was warm, his touch sending bubbles of nervousness throughout her. She was beyond attracted to the man. He nodded to the other ladies again and then escorted Hollie to the dance floor where he settled his hand on her hip and swept her into the crowd of dancers.

Holly had learned the two-step when she was young and she easily fell into the rhythm and pace that John set. He was a good dancer and soon she was thoroughly enjoying the moment. One dance led to another. By the third dance she was out of breath and her face flushed. She was glad when he pulled her away from the dance floor.

He put his hand at the small of her back as he guided her toward the bar. "What are you having?"

She looked at him and had to tilt her head because of his height. "Rum and Coke."

They took two empty stools at the bar and John ordered her drink and a Rolling Rock beer for himself. She felt suddenly shy when he turned his attention from the bartender to her.

He took her hand and caressed the back of it with his thumb. "How was the last day of school before the break?"

Startled that he'd taken her hand and almost too surprised to think, for a moment she couldn't think of a word to say. She thought about her class and then her stepbrothers. She chose to go with the part that made her feel good—her students.

"It was great." She smiled as she thought about her kindergarteners. "I have the best kids in the school."

He rubbed his thumb over her knuckles. "They have the best teacher."

His touch was distracting her. Still, she managed to say, "I don't know about that."

"I'm a good judge of character," he said. "And I think you're something special."

Heat rushed to her face and she looked down at their hands. She didn't know what to say.

The bartender set their drinks on the bar. With her free hand, she picked up her rum and Coke and took a healthy swallow. It burned as it went down her throat and as it hit her stomach she realized she hadn't eaten anything since noon.

She let out her breath and pushed aside her drink. "I need to get something to eat. It's been a long time since lunch."

From the bar top, John picked up a menu that was filled with the kind of bar food that was greasy and high in calories. She didn't care what it was, she just needed something to distract her from the way he was making her feel.

He handed her the menu. "What would you like?"

She shrugged. "Will you share with me?"

"I could use a little something to eat." He gave a nod. "The loaded nachos are always good here."

"They are." She set the menu down. "And they're huge. More than enough to share."

He caught the bartender's attention and placed their order. When John turned back to her, he said, "Now where were we?"

"Ah…" She tried to think fast. "I believe you were telling me how your day at work went."

"You can't throw me off track so easily." He grinned then sobered a little. "But I will let you know that talking about my day wouldn't be good for polite conversation."

"Fair enough." She picked at a fold on her jeans as she looked at him and wished she hadn't brought up his work. She'd been having such a good time she'd forgotten about her stepbrother being at the police station. She did wonder what he was in trouble for this time, but she wasn't about to ask John, or Carl, for that matter.

John squeezed her hand. "I don't know what it is about you, but like I said, there's something special about you."

Not knowing what to say, she bit the inside of her lip. Her eyes met John's, his gaze holding hers for what seemed like an eternity.

She got lost as she looked at him. His dark hair was cut short above his collar, his western shirt snug around his muscled biceps and chest. But it was his eyes that drew her in…pulling her closer and closer…

He looked upward and her gaze followed his. A sprig of mistletoe hung over them. His lips curved into a sexy smile as their eyes met again and she swallowed. "You wouldn't want to let that mistletoe go to waste, now would you?"

Words would not come to her and she couldn't look away from him. She caught her breath as his mouth neared hers…

Shouts shattered the moment and John jerked his head up, his attention immediately cutting to the commotion and his expression shifting so that it was now hard. Through their joined hands she felt the rigidity that was now in his body, which had been relaxed before now.

Next thing she knew, a chair flew through the air. It crashed onto the middle of a table, sliding into one of the four people sitting there. The man who'd been hit bolted to his feet and ran toward the crowd growing near the billiards tables.

The moment the chair hit the nearby table, John had released her, shot out of his seat, and charged into the melee. Shouts and cries gained volume and another chair spun and crashed too close to Hollie for comfort.

Heart pounding, she found herself hurrying away from the bar and rushing toward Leigh and Carilyn who sat in their seats wide-eyed as they craned their necks to see what was going on. Kelley was already out of her chair and headed toward the crowd. Considering she was on the police force too, it wasn't surprising that Kelley was getting in the middle of whatever was happening.

It took a few moments, but then the crowd backed away and Hollie's stomach pitched as she saw Kelley arresting two men Hollie didn't know...and John cuffing two of her stepbrothers, Dickey and Floyd. Their faces were bruised and their knuckles red, the skin split. The other men looked like they'd come out on the worst end, one with a bloody nose that hadn't stopped bleeding and the other whose eyes were swelling shut.

Hollie clenched her fists, her nails digging into her palms as she stared at John and her stepbrothers. Embarrassment, hot beneath her skin, caused her body to prickle and her chest to ache.

"I need to go." Hollie scooped up her purse that she'd left on the table. She withdrew her wallet from her purse, pulled out a twenty, and dropped it on the table. "Please give this to the bartender," she said before she grabbed the jacket off the back of her chair. "It's for the nachos we ordered."

"Stay." Leigh put her hand on Hollie's arm. "There's nothing you can do."

"I don't intend to do anything but go home." Hollie's lower lip trembled. "I'll see you later."

She looked straight ahead, not wanting to see John's face as she pushed her way through the crowd and hurried out into the night.

CHAPTER 5

*S*o much was spinning through Hollie's mind that she didn't think to put her jacket on. Blue and red lights flashed from the police cruisers stationed in front of the bar, the glow lighting up the windows and reflecting off of the cars in the parking lot.

When she reached her car, she fumbled with her remote and the cold door handle was like ice to her touch. Trembling from cold, she opened the door, climbed inside, and tossed her purse and jacket on the passenger seat. Her icy fingers had a difficult time sliding the key into the ignition but she made it and started the vehicle. She sat for a while, shivering violently as her car heated up. The shivering wasn't just from the cold. Anger at her brothers and humiliation also made her shake.

She had to fight back tears as she chewed one of her nails and waited for the cold to dissipate and for the heater to warm her body. John probably wouldn't want anything to do with her. He'd realize that she came with baggage in the names of Carl, Dickey, and Floyd. She was stuck in her position and there was nothing she could do for it.

As she sat there the pounding of her heart started to slow and she realized that she shouldn't be driving yet. Most of the alcohol she'd had to drink had worn off but she hadn't eaten anything for so long and she was lightheaded. She put her forehead against the steering wheel and closed her eyes. What should she do? She clenched her teeth. She'd have to stay in the warm car and wait for the police to leave, and then she'd go back in.

A knock came at her window, startling her into raising her head. The window was partially steamed and it was dark outside save for the intermittent flash of red and blue lights, so she couldn't tell who the dark form was as it peered in at her.

She quickly locked the doors, something she should have done to begin with. Who knew who was out there? It could be Floyd or any of her stepbrothers' other friends. The person knocked on her window again. She bit the inside of her cheek as she wiped away the steam with her sweater sleeve.

Her chest ached when she saw that it was John. For a moment she closed her eyes and did nothing. A moment later, she took a deep breath and buzzed down the window. Cold air flooded the car, chasing away the heat.

"Unlock the door and move over," he said.

She blinked at him but found herself obeying him without question and moved. When she was in the passenger seat, he climbed inside, shut the door behind him, and buzzed up the window.

For a long moment he looked at her, but she turned her head away. He captured her chin in his hand and turned her face so that she was looking into his brown eyes.

"Don't leave like that again." His voice was firm.

She looked at him in surprise, feeling like she wasn't hearing him quite right. "What?"

"There's no mistletoe in here." He slid both hands into her hair. "But as far as I'm concerned we don't need any." He brought his mouth down on hers.

She gasped in surprise as he took control, his lips moving

over hers in a firm, slow kiss. For a moment she was too stunned to move, but then she braced her hands on his chest, feeling the heat of his body through her palms as she kissed him back.

His unique, spicy, masculine scent filled her, making her want even more. All of her senses blazed...she reveled in his taste, the feel of his stubble against her face, and the calluses on his palms sensitizing her soft skin.

She didn't feel cold anymore. All she felt was the heat of his body, his presence wrapping around her like a cloak.

When he drew back and took her in with his gaze, she was barely conscious of grasping his shirt in her fists, wanting to pull him back to her for another kiss, wanting everything he could give her.

"Don't run away from me." He stroked her hair with his fingers. "Your stepbrothers may be bad news, but that has nothing to do with you and me."

"Me and you?" She felt confused and like she hadn't heard right.

"Maybe I'm rushing things." He wrapped a lock of her hair around his finger. "No, there's no maybe about it. I do know I'm rushing things. But I know what I want and follow my gut. I want to date you, Hollie. I want to get to know you. And I don't want those damned stepbrothers of yours getting in the way."

She swallowed, her mind spinning, refusing to accept what he had to say. "Why me?"

He shook his head as he stroked her hair. "Why not you? I told you I think you're special and I meant every word. I've been watching you for a while." When she raised her eyebrows he gave a little grin. "Not like it sounds. I haven't been stalking you. Every time I've seen you somewhere in public, I've wanted to talk with you. This morning gave me the excuse. Like I said, I know I'm pushing things too fast, but I know I want to get to know you better. A lot better."

"Oh," was the only word that she could get out.

"Say yes." He rubbed his thumb over her cheek as he looked into her eyes. "Say you'll agree to see me."

He had completely taken her off guard. "Wow." She knew it was lame and she blurted out, "I want to see you, too."

For having such harsh features, his smile was meltingly sexy. "I wouldn't have let you say no."

Her lips trembled as she smiled back at him. "Is that right?"

He gave a slow nod. "Yep."

Again he kissed her. It was the sweetest kiss she'd ever experienced. Not that she'd experienced many kisses, but his was amazing. It drew something from deep inside her, making it grow, filling her with a sweet warmth that she never wanted to let go of. This time when they parted, her breaths were uneven and so were his.

"One more thing," he said with a serious look.

She gave a little sigh. "What's that?"

"Were you planning on driving after having a few rum and Cokes?" he asked.

Her face burned and she looked at her hands that she'd dropped to her lap. "Once I got out here I realized that I shouldn't be driving and I was going to go back in after the police cars left." She looked out the passenger side window. "I was too embarrassed to go in right away."

"I get that," he said and sounded like he was choosing his words carefully. "Your stepbrothers are…not nice men."

"That's putting it mildly." She felt absolutely miserable talking about them. "You can say what they really are. You won't offend me."

"Let's not talk about those idiots." He put his hands on her shoulders. "As far as we're concerned, that trash will never come between us."

"Okay." Her lips trembled a little as she smiled. "That's a deal."

He gave her a grin. "Good. I'm going to hold you to that."

She smiled and he kissed her again.

It was a long time later that they came up for air. The windows were steamed and her body felt warm and ready for him. But she knew he wouldn't take advantage of her and she also knew she wouldn't be ready for a sexual relationship with a man she barely knew. Still, that didn't mean she didn't want him.

"I'll give you a ride home," he said.

She sobered. "That's the last place I want to be right now."

John frowned. "Do your stepbrothers hurt you...in *any* way?"

She thought about some of the things they'd done to her, how their friend, Freddy, made her worry that he'd sexually assault her. She thought about lying and saying no, that her stepbrothers did not abuse her, but she settled for a shrug. "They are who they are. I don't have a lot of choice in the matter."

The flash of anger in John's eyes startled her. His face looked tight. "I take that as a yes."

"It's verbal, John." She realized she'd said his name for the first time, and it felt natural. "They're just plain mean. They haven't physically hurt me."

"Verbal abuse is abuse, Hollie." The anger in his eyes magnified. "You need to get away from them. They're bad news."

"I don't have any choice." She glanced away from him and stared out the window. "They live with me."

"Who owns the house?" John asked.

"I do." She looked back at him. "They never left after their mama died."

"Then you do have a choice." John's voice was firm. "You can kick them out."

"I—I can't." Hollie bit her lower lip and felt a sharp pain before she spoke. "They've made threats. To be honest, I'm afraid of them and what they can do."

If she'd thought he'd looked angry before, it was nothing compared to the look on his face this moment. "My brother is the Yavapai County Sheriff," John said. "He can go to your ranch and order your stepbrothers to clear out of your place and get off your property."

Hollie felt miserable. "My stepbrothers are vindictive and they can get even with me. They have friends, ways of doing things that won't come back on them."

John sat for a long moment, clearly thinking over the situation. "Between you and me, I believe that they're up to something. I'm going to find out what it is, and I'll be the one to send them to prison for a good long time."

"I can only hope." She sighed. "In the meantime, I'll have to deal with them."

"Stay with me." He stroked her hair from her face. "I promise to be a perfect gentleman. Or if you'd rather, stay with one of your friends. Get away from your stepbrothers."

"I can't." She put her hand over his. "It's my home. Everything I own is there. I can't leave them to tear up the place or sell my things to get even with me for leaving." She clenched her hands in her lap. "Carl ordered me to cook dinner tonight and I refused, so who knows if I'll find my china shattered all over the house again." She shook her head. "I knew that when I refused he'd figure out a way to make me pay. But I just couldn't take seeing him or Floyd and Dickey. And if Freddy's there it will make it even worse." She shuddered. Truth was, Freddy scared the hell out of her.

John slammed his palm into the steering wheel. "I can't watch you go through this."

"It's the only way." She offered him a little smile. "I'll make it through this. I've lived with them for a long time now. I don't think it's going to get any worse than it is." At least she hoped not. And right now all she could do was hope.

John said nothing for a long moment. "We can't let you drive home even slightly intoxicated. Do you want to go to my house for an hour or two?" He held his hands up. "Scouts' honor that I'll behave."

"I'm not worried about that." She gave him a shy smile. "I trust you."

"On second thought, I don't know if you should." He brushed hair from the side of her face. "I'm more than attracted to you."

She put her hand over his. "I do trust you."

"Your car is warm," he said, "so why don't we leave my truck here and I'll drive your car to my house?"

"Let's go, Lieutenant," she said.

His grin was quick and sexy. "Buckle in, Teacher."

CHAPTER 6

$\mathcal{H}$ollie buckled her seatbelt as John put on his own. He shifted the car into gear and backed the vehicle out of the parking space and headed for the street. While he drove, he took her hand and held it on the console between them. She liked the feel of his hand wrapped around hers. How could she feel so unbelievably comfortable with him now? Her nervousness had ebbed with their conversation and his kisses.

She looked out the window at the Christmas decorations passing by in mostly red and green blurs. What a strange day. She'd gone through so many emotions and now she was with John. She'd had a mad crush on him and had admired him from afar and now he'd told her he wanted to date her...and they were on their way to his home until she was totally sober. It was strange how things could change in just a matter of hours.

It wasn't far to his neighborhood on the outskirts of town. Homes along his street were decorated with Christmas lights and displays that glittered and shone in the night. When they pulled up to his house, she saw that he lived in a modest ranch-style home.

"I think I expected you to live on a ranch like most of the other McBrides," she said before they got out of the car.

He shrugged. "I intend to go into ranching. I've just been waiting for the right time."

She blinked with surprise. "So you don't plan on staying on the police force?"

He opened the driver's side door. "I guess you could say ranching is in my blood."

She slipped on her jacket. Just as she grasped the door handle, John opened it for her. She grabbed her purse in one hand while he took her other and helped her out of the car. He locked the vehicle before wrapping her cold fingers in his warm ones and leading her to the front door of the house. Even though they would soon be inside his home, the biting cold had her wishing for gloves and a scarf.

It was too dark to get a good look at the outside of the house. When he let her inside, she breathed a sigh of relief as warm air met her. She liked this time of year, but it was good to get out of the cold.

When he closed the front door, he helped her remove her jacket and draped it over one arm of a chocolate brown leather sofa, and he set her purse next to it. He removed his own jacket that he must have put on after stopping the fight and arresting her stepbrothers and the other men involved. The thought of the fight and her stepbrothers soured her stomach so she shoved it away.

While he set his own jacket down, she took in his living room. It was done in warm colors with the brown leather sofa and loveseat, a caramel-colored recliner, and rugs of muted shades of browns and greens scattered on the hardwood floor. He had a built-in entertainment center with a flat screen TV and a stereo system. A few family photos were on the mantel of a fireplace that took up one corner.

"Give me a moment to make a fire." John went to the stack of wood beside the fireplace and he used kindling and small sticks to start the fire before adding bigger pieces of wood and a log.

When John turned back to Hollie, he saw her still shivering and rubbing her hands together. In a few steps he reached her then took both her hands in his and massaged them until she began to feel warmth starting to work its way through her fingers.

He lowered his head and pressed his lips to her forehead. "How does that feel?"

She nodded. "Better."

"But you're still shivering." He drew her into his arms. "Maybe I can help with that."

His body felt so good against hers that she felt his heat seeping into her bones. She pressed the side of her face against his chest and breathed in the smell of fresh winter air and his spicy masculine scent. A soft sound escaped her, a sigh of pleasure at the feel of his arms embracing her and the feeling of security that wrapped around her like a blanket. With him she felt like she could never be hurt by anyone again.

A false sense of security, no doubt. His job might be to protect and serve the community but it wasn't his job to babysit her and keep her stepbrothers and their friends from hurting her in any way.

She wrapped her arms around his waist and just let him hold her as he stroked her hair. "Feeling warmer now?"

"Yes." She tipped her head back and smiled at him. "Much warmer."

He studied her features so long that she felt her cheeks reddening. "You're beautiful, Hollie."

"You make me feel beautiful," she said softly.

"That's because you are." Slowly he lowered his head so that his mouth barely hovered over hers. When he spoke again, his warm breath caused her to sigh. "I think I've wanted to kiss you since the first moment I ever saw you."

Her throat worked as she swallowed. She'd wanted that too, but she was too shy to say so.

His lips met hers and he kissed her gently, slowly. She gave a soft moan and slid her arms around his waist, burrowing into his warmth and the long muscular length of him. It was as if she couldn't get close enough to him. She wanted to feel every part of him. To have his weight pinning her down, as if that might make them one.

He caressed her, sliding his palm over her figure as if he loved exploring her body. With him she didn't feel embarrassed by her generous curves. He slipped his other hand into her hair, grabbing a fistful and holding her head still as his kiss intensified. She loved the feel of her hair tight against her scalp, loved the feel of him taking control.

His kiss was like nothing she'd ever experienced before. His taste, a heady aphrodisiac on her tongue.

When he raised his head, he gently pushed hair over her ear. "Would you like something to drink? A mug of hot chocolate will help warm you up."

"You've warmed me up." She smiled at how easy it was to flirt with him. "But a mug of hot chocolate sounds good. Got any of those little marshmallows?"

"Of course. They're my favorite." He gave her a quick grin. "Just bought a package when I picked up the hot chocolate."

He took her hand and led her to a kitchen. It was a small, sparse kitchen with black speckled Corian countertops and black appliances. "Have a seat." He gestured to a round kitchen table.

As she sat on the edge of a chair, his cell phone rang. He drew it out of the holster on his belt and looked at the screen. He pressed a button to silence the ring and put the phone back in its holster.

He went to a pantry and withdrew a box of hot chocolate packages and a bag of mini marshmallows. "You didn't get a chance to eat those nachos," he said as he put water into a polished copper teakettle. "You've got to be even hungrier now."

She nodded, noticing for the first time since they'd ordered the nachos that she was lightheaded from being so hungry. "Yes. You could say that."

"Let me see what I have." He turned the heat on under the teakettle. "Can't promise I have anything fancy."

"I'll eat anything." She watched him as he went to the fridge and opened it. It did look pretty bare from where she was sitting.

He looked over his shoulder at her. "I've got hard salami, cheese, and crackers."

"Sounds great." She stood and rubbed her palms on her jeans. "I can help."

He set the packages of cheese and salami on the counter and grabbed a box of crackers from the pantry, then brought out a cutting board, a knife, and a couple of plates. She took over slicing the meat and cheese while he brought out a pair of mismatched mugs from a cabinet.

The teakettle whistled, steam shooting through the spout. He turned the heat off from beneath the kettle and set it on a cool burner. While she arranged the food on the plates and added crackers, he tore open packages of hot chocolate mix and poured them into the mugs before adding water. He stirred the chocolate before plopping marshmallows into the mugs and stirring the chocolate again.

She carried the plates of cheese, salami, and crackers to the table and he followed with the hot chocolate as they settled in seats across from each other. She picked up her mug and blew on the hot contents, breathing in the warm scent of chocolate before sipping from it. She closed her eyes as she rolled the chocolate over her tongue. The taste was rich and sweet and felt good siding down her throat to her stomach.

She opened her eyes to find John watching her. He had the

look of a man starved for something, but that look passed as their gazes met.

Heat from the mug warmed her fingers as she held it between her palms. "It's good," she said.

He drank from his own mug and set it aside before starting in on his plate of food. She watched him from beneath her lashes as he stacked cheese and meat on a cracker then put the whole thing into his mouth in one bite. She smiled as she took a small bite of the stack she'd made on her own plate.

It was quiet for a while as they ate. For a few moments she couldn't think of anything to say. When she finally did, she cleared her throat. "All of your brothers are in some form of law enforcement."

He nodded. "My stepbrother, Garrett, is a private investigator and my other stepbrother, Reese, is a detective. And I mentioned to you before that my blood brother, Mike, is the county sheriff."

"You get along with your stepbrothers?" she asked, thinking of her own.

"They're both standup guys," John said. "They're all good men."

"Did you always get along?" she asked.

The corner of his mouth curved into a smile. "I wouldn't say that. When we were young we had our fair share of fights. I don't think we really appreciated each other until we were adults."

"I wish I could say the same." She tried to smile and not to let any sadness or pain enter her voice. "I wasn't quite as fortunate."

John's expression darkened and she wished she hadn't said anything at all. "One way or another, I'm going to figure something out that will get them out of your life. For good."

"Right now I don't see how." She gave him a little smile. "Unless you're able to arrest them and send them to prison. But I doubt they've done anything bad enough to end up in prison." She frowned. "At least I don't think so."

John's expression darkened, but he said nothing. She had the feeling he had information about her stepbrothers that he was holding back. Likely he couldn't say anything because it was an ongoing case.

What kind of trouble could her stepbrothers be in now?

When they finished eating, Hollie wiped her fingers on a paper napkin and John carried their plates and empty mugs to the sink. It took only a few moments to wash, dry, and put away the dishes.

They returned to the living room. John took her hand and brought her down on the couch beside him. She kicked off her shoes and tucked her socked feet beneath her as he put his arm around her shoulders and pressed her head against his chest. He slid his fingers into her hair as she snuggled closer to him, feeling like they were two puzzle pieces that fit together. Maybe it was too soon to feel that way, but right now it did.

As she rested against him and he stroked her hair, she listened to the crackle and pop of the fireplace and found herself feeling drowsy. She relaxed more fully, lulled by his warmth, his scent... His body was solid, hard, yet she fit so comfortably against him... Warm and secure in his embrace...

She woke with a start. She was confused only a moment as she gained her bearings. She was lying on John's chest, his arm draped over her, caging her in.

Yet she didn't feel caged. She felt safe. Like he could protect her from anything, anything that the world had to throw at her. Including her stepbrothers.

She shifted and put her hand over her mouth to stifle a yawn.

"Awake, Princess?" he asked.

She moved in his arms so that she was looking into his eyes. "How long was I asleep?"

John glanced at his watch. "Two hours. It's close to midnight."

She raised her brows. "Two hours? You must be stiff from sitting here so long."

His shoulders lifted in a slight shrug. "Not really." His fingers slid down the length of her hair. "It's been nice."

"It has." She smiled at him.

"I think enough time has passed since your last drink," he said. "It's been a good three hours or so." He gave her a sexy little smile. "Unless you want to spend the night." He held up his hand. "I promise to be a real good boy."

"I trust you." She pushed herself to a sitting position. "But I do need to get home."

He shifted her so that she was sitting up. "I'll drive to the Highlander and we can get my truck before you head on to your place."

It took only a few moments to get their jackets on and for him to make sure the fire was out. Before they walked out into the chilly night, he handed her the purse he'd set on the couch.

He opened the passenger door for her. "Are you sure you're awake enough to drive home after we get my truck?"

She shivered. "If I wasn't before, I sure am now."

He kissed her on the forehead, helped her into the car, and closed the door behind her. She put on her seatbelt and rubbed her arms, trying to warm herself again. It had been so nice and cozy in his home.

Once the car was warmed up, he drove back to the bar. Before she could open the passenger side door, he caught her chin in his hand. "When I get out, you can slide on over to the driver's seat so that you can stay warm."

She looked into his eyes, unable to respond when she saw the intensity of his gaze that heated her from the inside out.

He cupped her cheeks in both hands and slowly lowered her face to his. His kiss was gentle, his touch delicate. It seemed like the kiss lasted an hour yet no time at all.

"I'd better let you get home." His voice husky, he drew away. "I can follow you to make sure you get safely there."

"I'll be fine." She rested her palm on his stubbled jaw. "Thank you for tonight."

"This weekend I'll give you a call," he said. "I have your number."

She smiled. "I'd like that."

He gave her another quick, hard kiss then opened the car door. Cold air rushed in and she scrambled over the console to get into the driver's seat. He looked at her one more time before closing the door firmly behind him.

The parking lot was still full of vehicles—the bar wouldn't close for another hour or so. John had parked her car next to a silver truck and she watched him as he went to it. The vehicle's lights flashed and then he climbed into the truck. Exhaust plumed from the muffler, rising into the night air.

Once he had started his truck, she backed out of the parking space and headed from the parking lot onto the street before driving out of town toward her ranch.

She smiled to herself as she drove, thinking about John and their first kiss. She thought about the time they had spent at his home and how he had let her fall asleep in his arms.

For a brief moment she thought about being under the mistletoe with him and that almost-kiss. But she found herself immediately pushing aside the thought because with it came the memory of how that almost-kiss had been cut short. That had been when the fight had broken out. She shook her head as she tried to rattle out the thought of her stepbrothers having been in a fight and how humiliating that had been.

She worried her lower lip as she thought about John and then she smiled. His kisses, his touch, and the way he had held her as she slept had been incredible. The fact that he wanted to see her again sent a thrill throughout her.

She knew that she was thinking like a dreamy teenager, but just maybe things would work out and this Cinderella would have her own happily ever after.

CHAPTER 7

*W*hen Hollie drove up to the ranch house, a lead ball landed in her gut when she saw Carl's beat-up old Ford truck in the driveway and Freddy's newer vehicle. Knowing that Freddy was inside her home made her belly feel as if it was filled with acid.

Freddy was crazy and he scared her even more than her stepbrothers did.

Both Dickey's and Floyd's trucks were gone, meaning they'd gone to the bar separately tonight. A thought flittered through her. Maybe Carl and Freddy had gone to town with Dickey or Floyd and she just hadn't seen either one of them at the bar.

She parked the car away from Carl's and Freddy's vehicles. She sat inside her warm vehicle for a few minutes, chewing a fingernail and staring at the house, praying that the two men were not inside.

"Suck it up and get in there, Hollie," she said aloud. "Don't let them get to you. They won't hurt you." She bit her lower lip. *At least not physically.*

But that thought was followed by another thought—Freddy had been making sexual comments to her for some time now.

What if he acted on them? What if he raped her, taking her virginity along with her dignity?

The acid in her belly climbed up her throat as she stared up at the older two-story home. If only there was a way to sneak into her house to avoid running into Carl or Freddy, she would gladly do it. Her bedroom was on the second floor and there was no way to get to it without going in the front or back door, and in either case she had to go up the staircase. The staircase's boards creaked and it was in the hallway between the kitchen and family room. Too bad she didn't have a sturdy trellis to climb up to her room.

Of course all she would be doing was delaying the inevitable, whatever the case. She had to face the men, if they were in there.

She let out her breath and shut off the motor. Immediately the warm air started to dissipate and cold began to creep in. She grabbed her purse, opened the door, and climbed out of the car before hurrying up to the front door of the house. Her hands grew instantly numb from the chill and she fumbled with her keys. She went ahead and tried the doorknob in case it was unlocked. Her heart sank as the cold knob turned in her hand.

The door squeaked as it swung open and she held her breath as she stepped onto the creaky wood floor.

"Is that the fat bitch?" came Carl's voice from the living room, his words slurring.

Great, he was drunk. She should be used to his verbal abuse by now, but it always stung, always chipped away at something inside her. Sometimes she felt so fragile that she thought she might break if they hit her hard enough with their words.

She stared around her. Pieces of china and shards of wood were scattered across the floor. Holes had been punched in the walls and the door to the closet beneath the stairs was hanging on its hinges. The contents of the closet were in a heap on the floor.

A hot and sick sensation filled her belly. She felt a wave of anger followed by despair as she set her purse down on the hall table and started to slip off her jacket. Carl stumbled into the entryway. Her arms were still caught up in the sleeves as he bore down on her, his features twisted and angry.

He caught her by the shoulders, her arms tangled in her sleeves. His breath was foul and smelled of sour beer. "I told you to get your fat ass home and fix dinner." Spittle flew from his mouth and felt like spots of acid when it landed on her skin. "You didn't do what I told you to and you come in late like this. I think you need to learn a lesson."

Her heart pounded as he gripped her arms tighter. "Let me go, Carl." She hated how her voice trembled.

He shoved her away from him so hard she stumbled. With her arms caught up in her jacket, she had no way to stop her fall and she hit the wooden floor hard, the landing jarring her teeth. She landed on wood shards and felt them through her jeans.

Carl nudged her hip with his boot just enough to make her grimace. "Get up."

The boot didn't really hurt her, but it still stung mentally. She tugged off the jacket, arms shaking with fury. She was scared, yes, but she was pissed, too. She said nothing as she pushed herself to her feet and hung her jacket on one of the coat hooks that were in a row along the wall by the door.

He grabbed her purse off the table and started digging through it.

"Give that to me." She put her hands on her hips, looking at him with defiance, but a tremble in her voice betraying her.

He sneered at her as he pulled out her wallet. He opened it and dug out the small amount of cash in ones and fives that she had left. He tossed the wallet onto the floor and counted the cash. "Thirty-eight fucking dollars?" He shoved the cash into his front pocket. "I know you've got something stashed around here. Where is it?"

She fought to keep her temper in check. "I don't have a stash."

"Bullshit." He took the three steps between them and then his face was in hers. "You always have one. Where is it?"

Freddy walked into the hallway, his smirk making her sicker. He leaned up against the archway that led to the living room as he watched. He was holding something in his hand that she couldn't see from where she stood.

"I'll get her to talk." Freddy ran his gaze over her in a way that made hair rise at her nape and her stomach churn.

"I've got this." Carl took whatever it was that Freddy had been holding and brought it closer to Hollie so that she could see it. Her heart hit the pit of her stomach. He was holding the old carved music box, inlaid with abalone and silver, a precious possession that her mother had passed down from their grandmother. It was one of Hollie's few remaining treasures. She'd kept it hidden beneath a loose floorboard in her bedroom.

"Where did you get that?" Her voice shook.

Carl laughed. "Been looking for the cash you've hidden and found this instead. Tell me where your stash is or I will break this piece of crap."

"No." Hollie reached for the music box. She couldn't give him the ten grand she'd hidden and she couldn't lose one of the last precious things she owned.

Before she could do anything, before she could think it through, he flung the music box on the floor and slammed his boot on it, crushing it beneath his heel.

Tears pushed from her eyes and rolled down her cheeks. She wanted to hit him like she'd never wanted to hit anyone in her life. She'd been raised to be like a southern gentlewoman, and she'd never raised a hand to anyone. But all that went out the window.

Without really thinking about it, she swung her hand and slapped Carl with everything she had. His head snapped to the side. Slowly he turned his head to look at her, fury and hate burning in his eyes.

Fear shot through her like ice-cold shards. She knew in that moment she had screwed up and she was going to pay for it.

Even though she was expecting something, she wasn't ready for it when he backhanded her and she screamed. She clawed at the air as she started to fall and her fingernails raked Carl's arm. He hit her again. This time the impact of his hand across her face sent her sprawling. Pain splintered through her head. Even more pain shot through her skull as she slid across the floor and skidded into the wall.

Stunned and blinded by pain, all she could do was stare up at him, tears flowing down her cheeks. She felt something dripping from her nose and over her lips and touched her hand to it. Her fingers came back sticky with blood. She could feel her face starting to swell, the pain from the slap and from her head striking the wall so intense that she could barely see.

Carl spit on the floor beside her, rubbing the deep scratches on his arm. "Lard-ass bitch. You ever touch me again and I'll make you wish you'd never been born."

She tasted the blood on her lips and used the sleeve of her light blue sweater to wipe it away. The sweater would be ruined but right now she didn't care. She'd never hated anyone like she hated Carl in that moment. She winced as the fleece rubbed across her lips and realized that one of her lips was split.

"Get up." He swung his boot and the hard toe connected with her side. She cried out as more pain burst through her. Had he just cracked one of her ribs? *"Get up."*

He turned away, leaving her sprawled on the floor. She blinked, nearly blinded by the throbbing in her head. She started to get up when Freddy stood over her.

She froze as he grinned. "You're like a broken doll, aren't you darlin'? Just waitin' for someone to pick up the pieces." He crouched down beside her and she held her arm beneath her nose, the sweater soaking with blood. He reached out a hand and trailed his fingers along her cheek. "I like to see when the light goes out of a woman's eyes when she's broken. It makes everything so much easier."

Her chest ached and she realized she was holding her breath as she stared up at him, afraid of what he might do. What if he did rape her like she'd feared? Carl would probably just watch and she'd see his hateful grin.

And John… If anything developed between them, he might not want her because she'd be damaged goods, ruined by Freddy.

Freddy was right, she did feel broken. She let out her breath. At that moment despair filled her soul and nothing had ever felt so bleak. She was trapped. There was nothing she could do, and now that Carl had crossed that line, there was no going back. Who knew how often he would hit her now.

She swallowed, still staring at Freddy. He trailed his fingers down the front of her sweater to her breast. She shuddered and flinched from his touch. He gave a low laugh, clearly pleased by everything that had just happened including the way she reacted to his touch. Sick bastard. "I like 'em big," he said.

"Let's go." Carl came up beside Freddy. "Dickey and Floyd went to the Highlander. We can go have ourselves a beer with them."

Hollie wasn't about to volunteer that his brothers had been arrested. Let them go and find out for themselves. No doubt she'd be the one bailing out Dickey and Floyd in the morning.

Carl glared at her one more time before he jerked open the front door and passed through the doorway. Freddy, who had still been crouched beside Hollie, got to his feet. He grinned at her then followed Carl out the door.

The moment the door closed behind the men, sobs wracked her body. She cried hard, not just for the physical abuse, but for all the things she'd endured at the hands of her stepbrothers.

Gradually she became aware that her palms were stinging. She looked at them and saw that pieces of wood and abalone had sliced into her flesh and were lodged there. She bit her lower lip as she started pulling out the splinters and shards.

When she finished, she pushed herself to her feet. Her face felt swollen from where Carl hit her, her head hurt from hitting the wall, her nose and ribs hurt, her eyes felt puffy from crying, and her palms stung.

She wiped away tears with her fingertips as she stumbled to the downstairs guest bathroom. Her heart sank as she saw more of her things broken in the bathroom. Carl had clearly searched for her stash in here, too. Everything was pulled out of the cabinet beneath the sink, the extra toilet paper and cleaners, and the cabinet above the toilet where she normally kept the folded towels. The towels were tossed across the bathroom and a bottle of shampoo was on its side on the floor, the shampoo dripping into a puddle.

When she went to look at herself in the mirror she saw that it was cracked in a diagonal line. Her reflection was distorted from the crack, but the blood on her swollen face, her blackening eye, and her split and swollen lip were only too clear to see.

She braced her hands on the porcelain sink, ignoring the sting in her palms as she lowered her head, closed her eyes, and cried.

When she thought she'd let loose every tear inside her, she found a clean washcloth and cleaned up. She wet the cloth and wiped tears and blood from her face. When the blood was gone, she picked up another cloth, wet it with cold water, folded it, and pressed it to her eyes.

A few moments later her eyes felt a little better and she hung the washcloth over the edge of the hamper along with the bloody cloth. She took a deep breath, side hurting, and shored up what strength she had. This time she didn't look in the mirror, not wanting to see the broken-looking woman staring back at her.

She stepped out of the bathroom and nearly stumbled over a lamp that lay in shards near the door. She wandered from room to room. It looked like the house had been ransacked. Her southern mother would have been horrified and would have made sure the house was spotless before retiring for the night. She couldn't dishonor her mother by leaving the house in such a horrible mess.

The thought of her mother gave Hollie strength. She got out the broom and dustpan along with a bottle of cleaning solution. When she started to clean the living room, she saw that something red had been spilled on the couch. She looked at it more closely and saw that it was ketchup. She found upholstery cleaner and worked out the ketchup before it could stain the material.

As she worked, her thoughts went over and over her day. She'd been so up and down emotionally that it was like being on a rollercoaster that never ended. Thinking about it only made it worse but she couldn't seem to stop.

When she finished with the couch, it occurred to her that Carl might have gotten hold of her cash, but more importantly, her family album. Praying she was wrong, she went to the coat closet by the front door. It had been emptied of its contents that were now strewn across the floor. The album wasn't in sight. Inside she located the sturdy panel that didn't move easily. It took some maneuvering to open it, but she'd done it so many times she didn't have a problem with it.

Her cash was stashed in a black bag back beyond the photo album where it was so dark it was almost impossible to see.

She'd hidden the cash, yes, but it was the album that was precious to her. She brought it out and sat on the floor, her back to the front door. She could hear anyone who might drive up and put the album away before it could be seen.

With a sigh she opened the album and a smile touched her lips as she saw her mom and dad's wedding picture. She gently touched the picture, tracing her mother's and father's outlines with her fingertip.

A lump lodged in her throat. Her parents had been so in love. Her father had been devastated when her mother died. When her father told her he was going to marry the woman who became her stepmother, Hollie had told him she didn't need a replacement mother. She was fine with her father to care for her and she cared for him. But he'd insisted that Hollie needed a woman's influence in her life. If only he'd listened to her—life would have been so much different.

For some time she looked through the photo album. She smiled as she looked at the photos of her mother laughing and her father smiling, and her own school pictures. She especially liked the photos of the three of them together.

A tear rolled down her cheek. This time it was for the loss of her parents. She missed them so very much. She carefully took a photo our of her mom and dad and tucked it into her purse to keep it close… And just in case her stepbrothers found the album.

After she put away the photo album, she cleaned the house, one room after another. In her room she found the floorboard moved that had hidden the music box. Not only had it been taken, but her small pistol that had been inlaid with pearl, a gift from her father, was also gone.

It had been late when she'd arrived home from John's, so by the time she finished cleaning, the sun was rising. She paused to look out her bedroom window, watching the glorious sunrise as pink and oranges spread across the horizon.

Exhausted, she lay down on her bed, hoping she could get in a little nap. But no matter how she tried, sleep would not come. She lay there, eyes wide open, her mind ruminating over all that had happened. The rollercoaster of emotions wouldn't stop—it was never ending.

With a heavy sigh, she rolled off the bed and onto her feet. She headed into the bathroom to take a shower and turned on the water to let it run until it was warm. She stripped out of her bloody snowman sweater, her bra, jeans, and panties. She'd already taken off her shoes and socks.

Once the water was warm, she stepped beneath it, tilting her face to the spray and letting the water wash away the feel of Carl's hand against her face and every other ugly thing that had happened.

Instead, she let her thoughts travel to John and how sweet and wonderful his kisses had been. She thought of how he'd looked at her, how he'd told her she was beautiful with such sincerity that she'd believed him.

She touched her fingers to her face and her lips trembled. John had told her she should kick her stepbrothers out of her home. Could she do it? Or would they beat her or something equally as bad?

Her body shook as she looked down. She hated that she was a coward when it come to her stepbrothers. She hated how beaten down they made her feel, as if every good thing in her life had been drained away and she'd never be happy again.

She clenched her jaw and turned her back to the spray. No, she was more than that. More than a broken doll to be thrown away and discarded. She raised her chin. There had to be something that she could do. Something.

Tired. She was so tired. Not just physically but mentally.

She let out a long, shuddering breath. It was a new day and she would figure this out. She had to. She couldn't live like this anymore.

CHAPTER 8

$\mathcal{I}$t was close to noon when Hollie headed to the police station to bail out Dickey and Floyd. Thank God Carl and Freddy hadn't come back. Carl was probably in town at Freddy's, drunk and sleeping it off. Just the thought of the two men sent a shudder through her.

Right now she was more angry than afraid. What she did know was that starting today, things were going to change. Things had to change if she was to survive.

Her palms stung from her wounds as she gripped the steering wheel. She pulled the car up to the police station and parked. She felt stiff and sore all over and her face and head ached.

When she shut off the car, she slid on a pair of big sunglasses that did a pretty good job of hiding her black eye. She let her hair hang long and loose, and it covered part of her swollen face. Nothing could be done for her split and puffy lip. There was no putting makeup on to hide it. She hoped she wouldn't run into John and that he wasn't working today. Even though she could hide her black eye with her sunglasses, she didn't want to explain why her face was swollen and her lip was split.

This would be the last time she'd bail out her stepbrothers. As a matter of fact, it was the last thing she'd ever do for them. She was ready to draw a line in the sand. She knew she could ask John or the sheriff for help but she intended to do it herself.

She climbed out of her car and despite the sweater and jeans she shivered. Over her car radio, the weather forecaster said to expect snow that evening. She liked the change of seasons, including snow, which was one reason why she was happy living in the northern part of the state as opposed to moving to the Phoenix area.

Sometimes she'd thought of leaving, abandoning all of the bad memories and starting fresh by selling the ranch and moving from Prescott to Phoenix or Tucson. But she had so many good memories here along with the bad. She couldn't let her step-brothers ruin it all for her.

Warm air chased away the chill as she stepped into the police station and closed the door behind her. Her sunglasses made everything seem somewhat dark and she wished she could take them off.

Considering the number of times she'd bailed out her step-brothers, she knew the procedure and didn't have to be told what to do. As she made her way across the station, her heart skipped a beat when John walked through a door.

Despite everything, she felt drawn to John in a way she'd never been drawn to anyone. His strength, his presence called to her. He looked so good in his uniform, so strong and powerful.

He smiled when he saw her, but immediately his smile faded and his hard features looked both concerned and angry. He headed toward her and was standing in front of her in a matter of a few strides.

"What happened?" His voice was as hard as his expression but his eyes were concerned. "Who hit you?"

She shook her head. "Don't worry about it."

"Like hell." He reached up and took off her sunglasses. He cursed when he saw her black eye and bruised cheek. His voice went low and even harder. "Tell me who did this, Hollie. Dickey and Floyd are here, so was it Carl?" When she didn't respond he swore again.

"I'm taking care of it." She eyed him steadily.

John's eyes were narrowed. If she didn't know that it was her stepbrother that John was furious with, and if she hadn't spent some time with him last night, she might have been afraid of him.

He cupped her face with his hand and lightly ran his thumb over her cheek. Even though his touch was feather-light, her eyes watered and she flinched. "This is not okay," he said. "You've told me that you're afraid of your brothers' retaliation. This isn't something you should handle yourself."

"I've made up my mind." She raised her chin and her gaze didn't waver as she met his eyes. "This is something I have to do."

John moved his hand away from her face, his jaw tight. "The sonofabitch assaulted you and you need to report it."

She shook her head. "Stop worrying about me."

"Damn it." He took her by the shoulders, gripping her firmly. "Don't be stubborn about this."

She said nothing and his expression made him look like his features were carved out of stone. His radio crackled and he put one hand to it but never took his eyes off of her. He responded to the dispatcher then removed his other hand from her shoulder.

"I have to leave." His tone was firm. "Stay here until I get back. We'll take care of it after I handle this."

She just watched him as he jogged to the door. He looked over his shoulder for one moment when he went through the door and then he was gone.

More determined than ever, she bailed out her stepbrothers but left before they could tell her they needed a ride. Their trucks were probably still parked at the Highlander and they could walk there as far as she was concerned.

Instead, she headed for the closest locksmith. She was going to take care of her problem and there was no stopping her.

. . .

JOHN SPED TOWARD THE SCENE, his lights flashing and his siren screaming. He needed to focus on the situation ahead of him but he couldn't help his fury over what Carl Whitfield had done to Hollie. John's anger was hot and liquid and he had to fight to contain it.

Hollie had looked so pale and fragile, like the wrong words could cause her to shatter. John ground his teeth, wanting to kill Carl with his bare hands.

John was the first to arrive at the house where the sound of gunshots had been reported. It was in a poor neighborhood without a homeowners association, the yard choked with weeds, and a rusted old car up on blocks in the street in front of the house.

Without his partner, John was required to wait for backup. Still, he climbed out of his cruiser, weapon drawn as he eased up the porch to the front door. The stairs creaked but he didn't hear any noises coming from the house.

When he reached the front door, he listened but still heard nothing. An unmarked vehicle pulled up next to John's cruiser. Reese and Will Carter. John waited for them to join him on the porch.

When they were in position, John called out, "Police! Open the door!"

Silence followed his shout. He reached out and touched the door, which creaked open without having to turn the knob.

John looked at Reese who nodded. John kicked the door open. "Police! We're coming in."

The smell of death hit him the moment he entered the house. John's gaze swept over the body on the floor, barely acknowledging it as he, Reese, and Carter first cleared room after room. When they determined the house was empty save for the body in the front room, John holstered his weapon and went to the dead man whose face had been blown off.

Carter searched the man's pockets but didn't find any ID. The one thing they did find was the tattoo on the side of the man's neck that told them he belonged to Jesus Perez's gang.

John dragged his hand down his face. "Too short and too slim to be Jesus. I'd guess this is Bobby Dominguez."

Reese nodded. "I'd bet you're right."

John reported to the dispatcher and it wasn't long before the coroner and techs arrived and the scene was being processed.

As he walked outside, his cell phone vibrated in his holster. He looked at the number, which looked familiar, but he couldn't quite place it.

"Lieutenant McBride," he answered.

"John," Hollie's hysterical voice came over the phone. It was a bad connection and he could barely make out what she was saying. "Carl...dead...my gun."

"Hollie?" he asked. He needed to make sure it was her since the connection was so bad.

"Yes." She sounded as though she was choked with fear and hysteria. "Carl. He's dead."

His gut tightened. "Where are you?"

"Home," she said with a sob.

"I'm on my way." He started to say something else but the connection cut out and then she was gone.

HOLLIE WAS COVERED WITH BLOOD. Carl's blood. She barely realized she was clenching her pearl-handled pistol and couldn't stop staring at his body and the pool of blood congealing beside him, and the smears across the floor. His sightless eyes stared at the ceiling.

She backed away from his body and against the wall. She slid down the wall and landed on the floor, never taking her eyes off of Carl. What had been Carl. The man who had backhanded her last night would never strike her again.

Her mind spun as she tried to grasp onto some form of reality. She finally looked away from his body and stared at the gun in her hand. It was covered with her bloody fingerprints. It wasn't a heavy weapon but right now it felt like a lead weight. Yet she couldn't drop it, couldn't let it go.

The horror filling her was like nothing she'd ever experienced before. Her mind was reeling, so much emotion that had bottled up inside her suddenly coming out in a scream as she stared at her bloody hands. Blood had soaked the cuffs of her sweater and there were smears across the front and on her jeans.

Everything was a blur and she couldn't think straight. Nothing made sense. What had happened?

She heard the sound of sirens but couldn't get herself to move. All she could do was look from the gun to Carl's body and back to the gun again.

The sounds of tires crunching on rocks in the driveway let her know that the police or sheriff's department had arrived. Probably the Yavapai County Sheriff's Department but maybe John. She had somehow managed to call John and he'd probably called the sheriff since they would have jurisdiction outside the city limits. John's business card lay on the floor beside her, a red thumbprint on the front of the card. She looked at her phone also lying on the floor and the bloody prints on the keypad.

Next thing she knew there was a banging at the door and she startled. Someone called out "Sheriff" and "We're coming in." Yet she didn't move. Couldn't move. All she could do was sit there.

A crash and the door burst open. Sheriff's deputies poured into the room.

One of them spotted her and pointed his weapon at her. "Put down the gun. Nice and slow."

She met his gaze. Frozen for a moment, unable to process

what he was saying. All she could see now was the barrel that was aimed at her.

"Put down the weapon," he said again. "Now."

The pistol slipped from her fingers and clattered to the floor. The deputy kicked it away from her and he lowered his weapon. "I need you to stand and come with me."

Dully, she stared at the officer and then noticed John behind the deputy.

When she saw him, she wanted to run to his arms and let him hold her and hope that he would never let her go.

"Hold on." John spoke to the deputy as he moved around the younger man. "I know Hollie."

The deputy frowned and looked like he was going to say something, but John moved past him. John was in uniform, wearing his badge.

"What happened, Hollie?" John said as he crouched beside her. "Is this Carl's blood on you?"

Slowly she nodded, her back still against the wall. "He was dying and I tried to stop the blood flow." Her voice sounded weak to her own ears. "But it was too much. There was so much blood... And I—I was too late to save him."

John rested his hand on her shoulder. "Did you shoot Carl?"

"What?" She looked at him, startled. "No. I would never shoot anyone."

"You were holding a weapon and it was pointed at the victim," the deputy interjected. "You're covered in blood and you're pretty beat up."

"It's my gun." Hollie gingerly touched her black eye with her fingertips as she turned her gaze from John to the deputy. "The pistol was lying in the foyer when I got home and walked in the front door. I didn't know how it got there, so I picked it up." She looked back at John. "I walked into the living room and saw Carl lying there...and the blood... God, there's so much blood..." She drifted off, still unable to process everything.

"Then what happened?" John prompted.

"He groaned and he looked at me, and he asked for help." Her throat worked as she swallowed. "I went to him and tried to stop the blood from leaking out of him." She shook her head. "Then Carl just died. Before I could do anything, he died."

"You said you just got home." John's features were unreadable. "Did you see anyone? Did you pass anyone on the road on your way home?"

"No one." She shook her head again. "Carl was the only one here and I didn't see any other vehicles once I got off the highway and turned onto the road to the ranch."

"What about on the highway?" John asked. "Did you notice any vehicles coming from the direction of your ranch?"

She strained to remember but nothing would come to her. "Maybe. I don't remember much that happened before I got here."

"Who gave you the black eye and split lip?" the deputy asked.

"Carl did." Hollie's throat felt raw as she spoke. "When I got home last night, close to midnight."

The deputy gestured to Carl's body. "Did you give him those scratches on his arm?"

She looked confused and turned her gaze on the body. "Yes." She looked back at the deputy. "When he hit me I started to fall and scratched him when I was catching myself."

"Did you kill him in retaliation for hitting you?" the deputy asked.

"I didn't kill him." Shuddering, Hollie rubbed her arms with her palms, feeling unbelievably cold. She started shivering violently.

"She's going into shock." John looked at the deputy. "She needs a blanket."

The deputy didn't move but called out to someone to bring a blanket. Hollie continued to shiver, feeling as if all the blood had drained from her body, just like Carl's blood had poured out of him. She barely felt the blanket that someone draped over her shoulders and arms. In her daze, she realized it was John.

"Sheriff McBride," the deputy said, his voice sounding far away.

Hollie and John looked up. John nodded to the sheriff, his brother, before turning his attention back to Hollie.

"We're interviewing a possible suspect," the deputy was saying to Sheriff Mike McBride. "Hollie Simmons, the victim's stepsister."

Suspect? Hollie blinked and looked at the deputy. With incredulity she said, "You really think I killed my stepbrother?"

John turned his gaze on the deputy, his eyes narrowed. He said something in a low, hard voice to the deputy, but Hollie was in too much of a daze to grasp the words.

The deputy looked angry and the sheriff stepped in. "I'll take care of this, Deputy Schmidt."

Schmidt steeled his expression, gave the sheriff a nod, and turned away.

"Tell me what happened," Mike said as he crouched beside John. Even though she was still in a kind of fog, Hollie found it easy to see the striking resemblance between the brothers, but there were differences. The main one was that John seemed more hardened and weathered than Mike did.

Hollie repeated the story to Mike. She found strength in John's presence as she spoke. She clenched her fingers when she told him about trying to stop the blood flow and realized that John was holding her hand, even though it was coated in dried blood. Mike asked her about her bruised and swollen face, and she explained that, too.

"Was anyone else here when Carl Whitfield struck you?" Mike asked.

"Freddy Victors was." She felt a wave of heat wash over her as she remembered the things Freddy had said to her. "He threatened me sexually."

John's hand tightened around hers so hard she winced.

"Carl also destroyed your property?" Mike asked.

She nodded. "He trashed the house from top to bottom. Destroyed so many of my things."

Mike glanced around. "You say it happened last night?"

"I spent hours cleaning it up," Hollie said. "I didn't stop until I finished, which was after dawn."

"Is the debris in the garbage from your home?" Mike asked.

She looked at him, puzzled. "Yes."

"You said the gun is yours," Mike said. "It's registered to you?" When she nodded he said, "How did it come to be in the foyer?"

"I don't know." She hesitated. "Last night when I got home, Carl and Freddy had torn the place apart, looking for money. They found my mother's music box in my bedroom, beneath a floorboard where I'd kept it safe for years." She let out her breath. "I kept my pistol in there, too. When I went to check to see if the pistol was still there, I found that it was gone. Carl must have stolen it when he took the music box."

When she finished giving him all of the information she could, Mike called to a forensic tech to test her hands for what he referred to as GSR, gunshot residue. The tech's face remained impassive but he said something low to Mike who nodded. The tech also did something to her fingernails, checking beneath them.

After the tech finished, she said, "Can I please clean up?" She looked down at her bloody clothing. "I need to take a shower."

"We're going to need your clothes," Mike said.

"Why?" She looked at him in confusion.

Mike gave a nod in the direction of Carl's body. "To compare DNA from what's on your clothing to the victim's and to check for gunshot residue."

"I already told you it's his blood," she told him. "And you can't possibly find residue when I didn't fire the gun." But when his expression didn't change, she said, "I'll go clean up in my room and put on other clothes."

John stood and held out his hand to her. "I'll go with you."

Hollie took his hand and let him help pull her to her feet.

"I'm going to have Deputy Betty Turner join you," Mike said. "We need a female in with Ms. Simmons."

Hollie started to ask why but clamped her mouth shut and led John and Deputy Turner up to her bedroom.

CHAPTER 9

*J*ohn frowned as he studied Hollie who sat half in/half out of Mike's sheriff's department SUV. Her feet rested on the running board, her purse in her lap. Deputy Turner had already searched the purse to make sure she wasn't carrying a weapon or anything else that might be deemed dangerous. Mike would take her in for questioning in a matter of moments.

Seeing her battered face caused anger to burn within him, no matter that Carl was dead.

She had cleaned up, her light brown hair pulled back in a ponytail and she wasn't wearing any makeup. The bruises and her split lip were dark against her pale skin and her eyes were a little glassy, dazed. She had put on fresh jeans, a turtleneck sweater, sturdy shoes, and was wearing a jacket with a woolen scarf to keep her warm. Her hands were stuffed in her jacket pockets.

He crouched in front of her, no one else nearby, as he tried to form the right words. "One of the last things you said to me about what Carl had done to you was 'I'm taking care of it,'" he said.

Her eyes widened and she looked at him. "You think I did it? That I killed Carl because he hit me?"

"No." He shook his head. "But if you said that to anyone else, it wouldn't be good for you, Hollie."

"I didn't say it to anyone but you." She touched her fingers to her bruised eye. "I'm sure of it. I hated Carl for what he did to me, for everything he's done to me, but I would never kill him."

"What did you plan to do?" John asked quietly.

She stared at him. "Well my plan certainly wasn't to murder him." She looked down at the purse in her lap. "I went to the locksmith and arranged for him to come out and change all the locks tomorrow. I figured that was a good first step. Then I intended to cut my stepbrothers off from my money. I won't pay to bail them out or give them money for any reason again." She sighed. "That's as far as I'd gotten in my plans."

John nodded. If the murder weapon was her pistol, this wasn't going to go well at all. She'd been at the scene, had been holding the weapon when the deputy arrived, had been covered in Carl's blood, and they had found minute traces of gunshot residue. The traces were so minute that they could have come from having her hands on the body or by handling the weapon after the fact. All of the blood on her hands could have affected the results, too.

The fact that Carl had hit her and destroyed her possessions would give her motive. Not to mention the years of verbal abuse that she'd mentioned. Was it just last night that she had told him about it?

Freddy Victors had witnessed Carl striking Hollie. Who knew what the man might say? For all John knew, Freddy had killed Carl and set up Hollie. They had to get Freddy in for questioning as soon as possible.

It could have been Freddy, but there was also the chance that someone from Jesus Perez's gang had killed Carl.

John turned to watch his brother, Mike, walk up to the SUV.

"We'll get on down to headquarters," Mike said to Hollie. "Watch your feet."

Hollie nodded and scooted onto the seat, bringing her feet in off of the running board. Her gaze met John's and he held it, not wanting to let the eye contact between them break. But then Mike closed the door, severing the connection.

"I'll meet you there," John said to Mike.

"What's your relationship with Ms. Simmons, John?" Mike asked.

"We were together last night." John blew out his breath. "Not sexually."

"You're clearly too close to her," Mike said.

Heat crawled up John's neck. "I'm going," he said. "I'll see you there."

Mike studied John, who cut his gaze away from his brother's. John turned and strode toward his cruiser that was parked in front of Hollie's home.

He looked back at Mike who was climbing into his SUV. In moments, Mike had started the vehicle and was driving back to the Prescott sheriff's department headquarters.

HOLLIE BURIED her face in her hands as she sat at the table in the room where the sheriff's deputies would be questioning her. At least they hadn't cuffed her to the table. They'd taken her in for questioning and hadn't arrested her.

She raised her head and leaned back in the chair as she waited for the deputies to come in. It was a nightmare, a complete and total nightmare. She couldn't say she'd mourn for Carl, but she would never have wished death on him.

The room was silent, sound muffled. She could hear blood pounding in her ears and she still felt numb, reality not quite sinking in.

She looked at the mirror and wondered if someone was

watching her now through the one-way glass. Something about being watched made her feel small, as if she was under a microscope. They probably had a camera on, recording her every move, her every expression. She didn't know what was going to happen next. Did they believe she didn't do it? Or was she truly a suspect?

It was ironic, really, that here she was in the sheriff's department headquarters when she'd been the one to pick up her stepbrothers from here or the police station so many times over the years when the brothers had been taken in for questioning or arrested. They'd been involved in bad things since they were young and she'd had to deal with it.

The door opened, startling her. Deputy Reg Schmidt and Deputy Betty Turner came into the room. Schmidt was unsmiling and had the same expression as he had when he'd questioned her at her home. Deputy Turner was the deputy who had accompanied Hollie to her room to clean up and change. The deputy had bagged up Hollie's clothes and had given them to a crime scene tech when they'd gone back downstairs. Turner's expression wasn't stern like Schmidt's, but it wasn't friendly, either.

Schmidt pulled up a chair directly in front of Hollie while Turner stood. Schmidt folded his hands on the tabletop and fixed his gaze on Hollie. "I need you to tell me exactly what happened," he said.

"I already told you everything." She felt thick, foggy, confused.

"We're going to go back through it from the beginning," he said.

"Okay." Her voice was small. He made her feel like a mouse about to be eaten whole by a cat a hundred times her size.

"Did you kill Carl Whitfield?" Schmidt asked.

Hollie clenched her hands in her lap, her nails digging into her palms. "No."

Schmidt looked her over. "How did you get the bruises on your face?"

"I told you," Hollie said. "Carl hit me last night."

Schmidt's expression didn't change. "Did you kill him in retaliation for hitting you?"

"No." Hollie shook her head. "I would never kill anyone."

Schmidt acted like he didn't hear her. "He came home, started pushing you around again, and you shot him in self-defense."

Hollie was so exhausted after over twenty-four hours without sleep and numb from shock. She had sharp pains in her head, her face hurt, her body ached. She didn't know how much more of this she could take.

"I did not kill Carl." A burst of anger shot through her. Schmidt was trying to rattle her, to take advantage of her exhaustion and shock. Her anger faded as quickly as it came. She was too exhausted to be angry.

"How do you explain the gunshot residue on your hands?" Schmidt said.

"The what?" Hollie stared at him.

Schmidt narrowed his eyes. "There was gunshot residue on your hands. Explain that."

Had there really been residue on her hands or was he trying to rattle her yet another way? "There couldn't be," she said. "The only time I've fired that pistol was at target practice and that's been years ago."

"So you know how to handle a gun," Schmidt said.

"Well, yes." She wanted to look away from his pale blue eyes. "My dad taught me when I was young."

Deputy Turner came up beside Schmidt. She spoke in a firm but kinder voice than what Schmidt had used. "Let's go back, Hollie. Tell us what happened from beginning to end," she said.

Hollie took a deep breath and told her story once again.

On the other side of the one-way glass, John gritted his teeth, his entire body tense with the desire to lunge through the glass and grab Schmidt by the throat. A part of John knew that Schmidt was only doing what John had done hundreds of times himself with the goal of getting the suspect's story under duress to see what might change, if anything.

Despite looking wan, exhausted, and still in shock, Hollie's core story never changed. But Schmidt tripped her up in places, drawing out what the brothers had done to her over the years and how that was a motive for killing Carl. She was clearly rattled, sounding more and more confused as the interrogation went on.

Hollie was innocent, damn it. John placed one fist on the window, bracing himself. After all her stepbrothers had put her through, now she had to go through this. He didn't remember ever feeling so frustrated, so angry, and so helpless.

"Maybe you should leave." Mike's voice came from behind John. "Like I said before, you're too close to this one."

John wanted to tell his brother to fuck off, but ignored him instead, staring intently at the scene before him as the deputies' and Hollie's voices came over the speakers.

A tech stepped into the room with John and Mike and held up a report. "Got the results back on the clothing. No gunshot residue on her clothing. What was on her hands could easily have come from handling the gun or touching the wound." The tech glanced at the report. "The blood on Ms. Simmons' clothes is a match to the victim's and she had his DNA beneath her fingernails. The only prints on the weapon belong to Hollie Simmons."

Mike took the report from the tech. "Thanks, Milo."

Milo gave a nod and left back through the door he came through.

John dragged his hand down his face. The fact that no residue was on her clothing was big, but they had found the trace residue on her hands. The other factors were enough for them to book her.

"Dickey and Floyd Whitfield are here," Mike said. "They've been put into separate interrogation rooms."

John let out his breath. He wanted to see their interrogations but he didn't want to leave Hollie, even if all he could do was watch.

"What about Freddy Victors?" John asked.

Mike shook his head. "He hasn't been located yet."

"This could have been a retaliation murder," John said. "We think Victors is responsible for picking off three of Jesus Perez's men, including Perez's brother."

"Why don't you get me what you can on those killings," Mike said. "Just maybe we'll find something that will tie Perez to Carl Whitfield's murder."

John's phone vibrated in his holster and he pulled it out and looked at the caller ID screen. It was Nadia. He frowned. Considering the nature of their friends with benefits relationship, it wasn't like her to call him often but this was the second time. She'd called him last night when he'd been with Hollie at his house and he'd sent Nadia's call to voice mail.

Well, he didn't have time to deal with her right now. He sent her to voice mail again.

John looked back to watch Hollie and his chest hurt to see her so pale, so beaten down by the deputies. She was innocent and she was being treated like a criminal.

He was going to do everything in his power to find the bastard who had killed Whitfield and put him away. Permanently.

CHAPTER 10

$\mathcal{H}$ ollie was almost too numb to realize what was happening as they booked her for suspicion of murder. The whole thing was surreal, like it was happening to someone else. How could this be happening to her?

Humiliation made her skin burn as she was cuffed like some dangerous criminal, patted down, then fingerprinted. This was beyond the humiliation she'd felt when she'd had to bail out her brothers from jail. Now she was the one going to jail. The reality was she could end up in prison if a jury determined there was enough evidence that would make them sure she was guilty.

Hollie had to fight back tears as her mug shots were taken. She'd lived with criminals, had suffered from their cruel words and actions. The police considered her a criminal now. Even if she was proven innocent, this was a stain on her life that could never be cleaned away.

The entire time she was being booked she didn't see John. Her heart hurt. Did he think she was guilty now after hearing every accusation against her?

She kept her head bowed as Deputy Turner took her to a cell and removed Hollie's cuffs. Three women were already in the cell that Turner opened. The deputy held the door open and Hollie stepped inside. The door clanked shut with a finality that sent a shudder throughout her body.

The cell had a toilet, a sink, and two bunk beds. One of the women in the cell had short dark hair buzzed at the sides and combed back on top, her expression hard and mean. A sick scared feeling churned in Hollie's belly and she avoided the woman's gaze. Another woman, who looked younger than Hollie, was leaning up against a concrete wall. She was squirming and brushing her hands over her arms as if snakes or centipedes covered her body and she was trying to shake them off. She made fearful helpless sounds that added to the sick feeling inside Hollie. The third woman lay on the bottom bunk of one of the bunk beds, staring up at the bed above her.

Hollie looked away from the women and retreated to a corner. Her legs gave out on her and she slid down the bars, finding herself sitting with her knees drawn up to her chest. She wrapped her arms around her knees and let her hair fall over her face in a curtain.

Moments later a shoe against her hip prodded her. Slowly, Hollie looked up to meet the mean gaze of the woman with short hair On closer look, Hollie saw she had a red spot that was likely a hole in her lower lip, a pair of red spots for holes through an eyebrow, a spot of red on her nose, and holes in her ears. She obviously normally wore earrings and facial jewelry that had likely been removed when she was booked.

"Whad'ya do?" the woman said in a heavy redneck accent.

Hollie knew she had to answer even though she didn't want to talk. "They think I killed my stepbrother."

The woman smirked. "I suppose you're innocent."

"I didn't kill him." Hollie knew she shouldn't show any weakness by crying, but she was having a hard time holding tears back.

"I'm Gert." The woman crouched beside Hollie and pointed at

the squirming woman. "That's Amber. She's in here for selling crack and she's got the DTs." She inclined her head toward the woman on the bed. "The bitch on the bed is Mary and she killed a family of four while driving drunk." Gert focused her attention on Hollie. "What's your name?"

Hollie swallowed. "Hollie."

"Well, Hollie. You look too goody-goody for your own good." The woman's face was unreadable. "What'd you do for a living?"

Hollie's shoulders sagged. "I'm a kindergarten teacher."

"We've got ourselves an innocent kindergarten teacher here." Gert raised her voice. "What should we do with her?"

Fear caused Hollie's heart to slam in her chest. Amber still squirmed against the wall, brushing away imaginary things crawling on her body. She had a wild-eyed look and continued to mutter under her breath things that made no sense.

Mary, who was lying on the bunk, turned her head and stared at Hollie in a way that made her skin crawl. Hollie felt like the woman against the wall must feel as she fought unseen creatures.

"You could use a friend, couldn't you, Teacher?" Gert drawled, bringing Hollie's attention back to her.

Hollie didn't respond and bit the inside of her lip. She winced at the pain from her split lip.

"Friends are hard to come by around here." Gert's eyes roved over Hollie. "But I think you and me could be friends. Real good friends."

"Why are you in here?" Hollie's voice sounded tiny as she asked the question.

Gert's eyes darkened. "Cops think I killed the woman screwing around with my girlfriend."

"Did you?" As soon as she said the words, Hollie wished she could take them back.

But Gert laughed. "Hell no. We're all innocent in here."

Hollie looked down at her knees. Gert was lying. Hollie had no doubt about it. A murderer was asking her if she wanted to be friends. Hollie didn't know what kind of friends she was talking about. Gert liked women—what if she raped Hollie?

Gert nudged her again, this time the back of her hand against Hollie's arm. When she looked at Gert, the woman was scowling. "You'd better think hard on your answer."

Hollie swallowed as she forced herself to say the words. "Yes. We can be friends."

"Good girl." Gert sounded pleased. "An innocent little kindergarten teacher like you won't last long in a place like this. You'd better hope you don't end up in Florence 'cause you won't have me to take care of you."

The door into the jail opened and Hollie and Gert looked up. Hollie felt a combination of humiliation and relief to see John. He gave Gert a hard look but the woman didn't back off.

Hollie found herself getting to her feet and she gripped the bars as she looked at John who was wearing his uniform and badge. He looked so good but so unattainable, his expression hard.

He turned his gaze on Gert. "Give her some space."

Gert smirked and walked across the cell, leaned against the wall, and folded her arms across her chest as she stared at John and Hollie.

Hollie's lower lip trembled as she looked up at John and she fought back tears. "I didn't do it, John." She didn't know why she felt like she had to convince him, but the words forced their way out.

"I know, honey." His voice was low and his expression softened. He looked like he wanted to take her into his arms but had to hold himself back. "We'll get the real killer, Hollie. In the meantime you'll get out on bail as soon as the judge sets it."

"What if he won't allow bail to be posted for me?" Hollie asked, her eyes burning now.

"You're not a flight risk." John put his hands over hers where they rested on the bars. "It's going to be all right."

She couldn't look at him and lowered her head as a tear leaked down her cheek.

He reached through the bars, caught her by the chin and raised her head. He wiped away the tear with his thumb. "You're strong, Hollie. Stronger than you feel or even know."

"Am I?" she whispered. "I don't feel that way. Not at all."

"Yes." He said the words firmly. "You are."

The way he said it made her feel stronger, at least in that moment.

"I'm sorry but I've got to go." His hands were over hers on the bars again. "I'll be back when I can. I promise it won't be long until you're out of here. In the meantime, you're going to be strong," he repeated. "Okay?"

She wished with all her heart that he didn't have to leave but nodded. "Okay. I will be." She didn't know if she believed her own words. Could she be strong?

"That's my girl." He squeezed her hands before turning away and going back to the main door that the female jailor opened for him. He looked over his shoulder and met Hollie's gaze, giving her a look of strength. A look that for one moment made her feel like everything was going to be okay. And then he was gone.

"You screwin' a cop?" Gert moved up beside Hollie.

"No." Hollie felt a rush of heat. "We haven't."

Gert snorted. "Sure."

Hollie didn't bother to argue with Gert. It didn't matter what the woman thought. Or did it? Gert might hate cops. Still Hollie said nothing.

Gert slapped Hollie on the shoulder. "I bet he's right and you'll be out on bail."

"I used up most of my remaining money bailing out my stepbrothers." Hollie's stomach churned again. "I might not have enough."

"Who are your stepbrothers?" Gert asked.

"Floyd, Dickey, and Carl Whitfield." Hollie swallowed. "Carl's dead. Someone killed him earlier today."

Gert whistled. "Good old Whitfield brothers. They think you murdered that asshole, Carl?"

"Yes," Hollie said.

"Can't say he didn't deserve it if you did," Gert said.

"I didn't." This time Hollie said it more defiantly.

"Whatever." Gert slapped Hollie on the shoulder. "At least you've got a cop on your side."

Hollie grimaced at the force Gert used when she'd hit Hollie's shoulder, but she said nothing. She could only pray that Gert was right and John could help prove her innocence.

CHAPTER 11

*H*ollie almost crumpled into a heap as the judge set bail. It was staggering. She didn't have that kind of money and didn't have enough collateral—there was still a mortgage on the ranch and she owned nothing else of value.

The public defender, Jason Dugan, stood at her side and put papers back in his briefcase. He seemed almost indifferent to her, like he had better things to do. Maybe he was just preoccupied with something personal. She wished she could afford an attorney who would be more invested in proving her innocence.

She was almost too numb for tears by now as she was cuffed again and escorted out of the courthouse, her hands behind her. The moment they stepped outside, she was struck by a feeling of horror. A crowd was waiting at the foot of the stairs and she realized they were reporters. For a moment she stood rigid with shock as questions were fired at her.

"Miss Simmons!"

"Did you kill your stepbrother?"

"Did Carl Whitfield abuse you? Was this a revenge killing?"

"Why did you kill him?"

CHEYENNE MCCRAY

"They're calling you the Killer Kindergarten Teacher. What do you think of that?"

Hollie's mouth felt dry and her chest hurt. She thought her knees might give out on her as blood drained from her face.

The public defender, on the other hand came to life, as if a switch had been thrown. Now he was clearly interested as if he'd suddenly realized that this would be a high profile case. Proving the Killer Kindergarten Teacher innocent would make for good publicity.

Jason gripped her upper arm in a firm grip and started to move her down the steps, through the mass of reporters. "Ms. Simmons has no comment," he said several times as they made their way.

She hung her head, hiding her face behind her long hair as Jason made a path for them through the crowd. Of course it was too late to matter—they'd already had plenty of time to take pictures of her as she came out of the courthouse and had been struck dumb. Her picture would be on the front page of the daily newspaper.

KILLER KINDERGARTEN TEACHER

The words went around and around in her mind. Her kids, her wonderful kindergarteners. What would this do to them when they saw that their teacher was accused of murder? They were young, but they would realize something bad had happened. No matter what the outcome was, there would always be the doubt in some people's minds...her reputation would forever be tarnished.

And what about her friends? What would they think of her?

Jason and a deputy escorted Hollie to the waiting deputy's car and opened the back door. She ducked down and slid onto the seat before the deputy shut the door firmly behind her.

She leaned forward on the seat, her wrists cuffed behind her, and the tears came, hot, like every one of them was burning a trail down her bruised face. The drive to the sheriff's department headquarters wasn't far and some of the reporters beat them there. Hollie was led up another set of stairs and into the head-quarters, her head down, her hair hiding the tears rolling down her cheeks.

"HOLLIE SIMMONS."

The female voice calling Hollie's name caused her to jerk her head up. She was sitting in the corner again, her eyes puffy from crying silent tears. She hadn't been able to stop since she'd left the courthouse. She slowly got to her feet and wiped her eyes with the backs of her hands.

"Bail's been posted for you." The jailor opened the cell door. "You're free to go for now."

Stunned, Hollie stared at the woman. She couldn't imagine who would have paid enough to post bail. "Who posted it?"

"No idea." The woman jerked her head, indicating Hollie needed to exit the cell. "Just be glad someone did."

Hollie couldn't help looking back at the women in the cell. Gert and Mary were staring at her. Amanda was sitting on the floor rocking back and forth and muttering beneath her breath.

Gert smirked. "See you later, Teacher."

Hollie bit her lower lip and turned away. She hoped with all her heart that she wouldn't be seeing any of the women again.

She was taken to retrieve her belongings, which included the purse she had taken with her the night she was taken in for ques-tioning, her driver's license, wallet, earrings, and cell phone. Her hands trembled as she placed everything in her purse. She was given her coat and the scarf she'd worn when she came in for questioning. She shrugged into the coat and wrapped the scarf around her neck. The whole time she felt dazed, as if this weren't real and she was still locked up and was hallucinating.

As she pushed open the door and walked out into the overcast day, she braced herself for more reporters then blew out a breath of relief. Thank God there were none. Likely they didn't know bail had been posted and had no reason to be there right now. They'd gotten their photos anyway when she'd left the courthouse.

At the foot of the stairs she saw John, his hands shoved into the pockets of the suede western jacket he was wearing.

Instead of his uniform, he wore plain clothes, including a black T-shirt pulled taut over his muscular chest that showed through the opening of his jacket. Wrangler jeans were snug against his thighs, and he had worn brown leather boots on his feet. A Stetson shaded his eyes and she couldn't read his expression.

Her body trembled as she walked down the steps to meet him. The moment she neared him, he reached out and pulled her into his arms, enveloping her in a firm embrace.

Everything she'd been holding back broke loose and she cried against his chest, hard, body-wracking sobs. She'd cried during her ordeal, but nothing like this. He rubbed her back with his palm as he murmured soothing words in her ear. She couldn't focus on what he was saying but the low rhythm and the tenor of his voice helped to calm her.

His words came to her as her tears dried and she let out a deep shuddering breath. "It's going to be okay, honey. We'll fix this. Everything's going to be all right."

She became aware of his warm scent of spice and leather, and the clean scent of his T-shirt that was so soft against her cheek. The cloth was damp from her tears.

Slowly she raised her head and looked up at John. "Did you post bail for me?"

He nodded. "When I heard you didn't have enough to do it for yourself, I worked things out with a bail bondsman. I had to get you out of there."

Guilt stabbed her but at the same time she was so relieved to be out of jail that all she could really be was grateful. "Thank you," she said. "Thank you." She didn't think she could say it enough times. "I've got ten thousand stashed at the ranch. I can give you that."

"Don't worry about that right now." He brought her against his chest again and slipped his fingers into her hair. "Come on. We'll go to my place." He put his arm around her shoulders and guided her toward a parking lot.

"Okay." She wasn't going to argue. She wanted to get as far away from the jail as she could as long as it wasn't her ranch house.

He helped her into the passenger side of the truck and closed the door behind her before going to the driver's side. He climbed in and started the truck. He rested his hand on the top of the steering wheel and reached across the console to take her hand in his free one. He squeezed.

She gave him a smile that she knew had to look sad because she couldn't manage a real smile.

"It's going to be okay, Hollie." He gripped her hand firmly. "We'll get whoever did this and clear your name."

She desperately wanted to believe him. "Okay."

He leaned close and kissed her forehead before backing the truck out of its space and heading out of the parking lot.

Her thoughts turned to her friends as he drove. Detective Kelley Petrova McBride had stopped by and told her that her friends, Leigh Monroe and others, wanted to see her. Hollie had said a flat "no." She was too embarrassed and too exhausted from the ordeal to see anyone. What if this made them feel differently about her? What if they had doubts about her innocence?

This time when they reached John's home it was during the day, unlike the first time that now seemed so very long ago.

His house was a single-level brick home with grass that was yellow now that it was winter and trimmed close and neat. The mature trees in front of his home had lost most of their leaves, their naked fingers pointing toward the sky. Yellow leaves were scattered around the base of the trees but very few, telling her that he had kept them raked up.

He parked the truck in the driveway and strode around the truck to help her out. She was grateful for him, needing his strength now, more than she'd realized.

When they were in the house, he took her scarf and purse and set them aside. He helped her out of her coat and draped it over an arm of the chocolate brown sofa.

"I need a shower." She was dying to get out of the clothes she'd been wearing for forty-eight hours now. "Can I take one here?"

He gave a nod toward a hallway. "You've got it."

She followed him, feeling bone weary and like she could sleep for a week. He led her into the master bedroom.

He pulled open a drawer, drew out a white T-shirt, and handed it to her. She took it and watched as he opened another drawer and brought out a pair of dark blue boxers. "These will be big on you, but maybe they'll do until we can get your own clothes."

"Thank you." She grasped the boxers in her fist then held the clothing to her chest. He led her into the bathroom. She watched as he turned on the shower and let it run until it was warm and steam started to build in the bathroom.

He handed her a thick blue towel and a toothbrush that was still in its package. "Just bought the toothbrush. Use whatever I have that you need." He kissed her gently before closing the bathroom door and leaving her alone. She was glad for the privacy. She'd had none while she was in jail and it was beyond words how grateful she was to be out. She owed John more than she could ever repay. Now she had to prove herself innocent. She didn't know how to do that and could only pray that John could.

A shower had never felt so good. As she soaped herself beneath the warm spray, the filth of the last forty-eight hours slid off her body. Even after she washed her hair, she still didn't quite feel clean enough. It was as if the experience had tainted her in ways she couldn't begin to express.

She realized she hadn't been chewing her nails like she normally did. It was as if everything in her life had changed and not for the better. She felt too numb to chew her nails.

After she got out of the shower and turned off the water, she dried off with the blue towel John had handed her before he left. She dressed in the T-shirt and boxers, both loose on her but comfortable. She gratefully brushed her teeth and then combed the tangles out of her wet hair.

When she was finished, she opened the bathroom door. Steam escaped the room as she walked into the bedroom. She looked at the bed that invited her to slide between the sheets like a lover beckoning to her. Without consciously thinking about what she was doing, she headed straight for the bed and crawled into it.

The bed smelled of John, a scent that wrapped itself around her and made her believe for a moment in freedom.

She rested her head on one of the pillows and drifted off to sleep.

CHAPTER 12

*J*ohn gritted his teeth as he almost slammed the phone receiver into its cradle. He was sitting at his desk in the police station, following up on whatever leads he could generate.

Hollie was innocent. He wanted to beat the shit out of whoever had killed Carl Whitfield and left Hollie to take the blame. It had to be Freddy Victors. The man had been missing, likely had gone into hiding, after murdering Carl.

When John had left this morning, Hollie had still been sleeping. He'd had to get to work, so his mother had come over to stay with Hollie so that she wouldn't be alone when she woke up. His mother was to alert him if anyone came near the house.

He thought about how exhausted Hollie had looked in her sleep, the dark circles under her eyes, and her pale, bruised features. He'd wanted to stay there and hold her until she woke, to be there for her. But he had to find the real killer and he couldn't do that without the resources he had at the station.

God, he'd never felt this way about any woman. He'd known he was getting in over his head when he'd asked her to dance at the Highlander. He'd only gotten deeper and deeper from that point on. What happened to staying away from relationships while he was a cop? What happened to waiting until he was ready to walk away from the police force and start his ranching career?

Because women like Hollie only come around once in a lifetime.

John's gaze moved to his computer monitor and he stared at the mug shot of Hollie. She looked tired, frightened, and as if she was about to cry. His gut clenched as he scrolled through her vitals and the evidence against her. He didn't think for a minute that she was guilty, but things sure looked bad. He had to prove her innocence before she went to trial. Hell, he needed to do it now. Her life, her career, could be destroyed by this if it weren't already ruined.

Killer Kindergarten Teacher.

Fuck.

He dragged his hand down his face, over the rough stubble, as he leaned back in his chair. He had to find Freddy and soon.

Jamie Cruz, John's young new partner, was back and doing well considering how deep the dog bite had been. Jamie looked up from the report he was filling out via his desktop computer. "No luck?"

"Not one damned clue." John had put everything he'd been investigating on hold to work on Hollie's case. Captain Johnson was allowing some leeway, but there was only so much time that John could spend on it.

His cell phone rang and he un-holstered it, hoping it was his brother Reese, or his stepbrother Garrett, with good news.

Instead he saw Nadia's name and number on the display. He frowned. This was the fourth time she'd called. She'd also sent several "call me" text messages. This was new behavior for her and he wasn't sure what to make of it. Maybe she was in trouble.

Still frowning, he answered, "Nadia?"

"Why haven't you been answering or returning my calls?" she asked in such an angry tone that it took him back for a moment. "Why haven't you responded to my text messages?"

John blew out his breath. "I don't have time to talk. I'm at work and I have a heavy caseload."

She ignored his statements and cut through what he'd said. "It's been three weeks since you were here last. When will I see you again?"

Hair at the base of John's neck pricked. "I'm at work and I can't talk. I'll call you later." He disconnected the call before she could respond.

With a grimace, he shoved his cell phone back in its holster. Nadia had apparently become attached to him despite her agreement that their relationship was strictly "friends with benefits." He should have known better, damn it. Should have known better than to believe a sexual relationship with one woman wouldn't lead to expectations he wasn't ready for and hadn't wanted. When he got off work he'd have to give her a call and end it.

"Everything okay?" Cruz asked, drawing John's attention to him.

"Fine." The word came out clipped and rougher than he'd intended, but he didn't make excuses for his sharp bark.

Cruz just nodded and went back to his report.

John picked up the receiver for the landline and dialed Garrett's phone number. Garrett was one of John's stepbrothers and a damned good PI. What a difference between his own step-brothers and Hollie's. They couldn't be more different.

"What's up, John?" Garrett answered, clearly looking at his caller ID screen.

"Any progress?" John asked.

"I'm calling in every favor that's owed to me." Garrett made a frustrated sound. "So far, not a damn thing. Freddy Victors might as well be a ghost."

"He's not that good," John muttered. "He must have someplace close where he's hiding out. I doubt he'd leave Prescott. He's just laying low, waiting for Hollie to be put away for Carl's murder."

"Could be," Garrett said. "I take it that you haven't had any luck finding Jesus Perez."

"As soon as I locate Perez, I'm going to haul his ass down here." John scowled. "I'd like to know where the fuck these bastards are hiding out."

"John, I've got Reese on the phone." Jamie Cruz held a cell phone as he interrupted John's conversation with Garrett. "Speaking of that sonofabitch, Reese and Carter located Perez."

"About damned time," John said. He repeated the information to Garrett before he added, "I'll call you back."

To Cruz, John said, "Do they have Perez in custody?"

Cruz shook his head. "They're waiting for backup to go in."

"What's the address?" John asked and Cruz gave it to him.

John gave a nod. "Tell Reese and Carter we'll be right there."

Cruz raised his cell phone to his ear and started speaking to Reese again while John disconnected the call. He pushed back his chair and surged to his feet, knocking over his chair in the process.

Brad Johnson, a rookie and a nephew of the captain, gave John a look that said, "What the hell's going on?" without voicing it aloud.

Narrowing his eyes, John glared at Brad who shrugged and went back to whatever it was that he'd been doing.

Cruz's legs weren't as long as John's but he kept up with John's pace. They reached the cruiser at the same time and climbed in, John on the driver's side. He drove out of the parking lot and headed toward the address Reese had given Cruz.

It took them ten minutes to reach the street the duplex was on. Reese and Carter were parked a few car lengths down the street.

Cruz accompanied John to the front door. Reese and Carter went around back. John knocked on it and said, "This is the Prescott Police Department. We'd like to talk to Jesus Perez."

A huge crash sounded inside and then a man jumped out the side window, dropped to the street, and started running.

"Oh, hell no." John took off after the man who was wiry and fast. The man's build was about the same as Jesus Perez's, but John couldn't be sure it was him.

Cruz joined in the chase as they jumped over fences, sped across streets, dodged vehicles, and ran through yards.

The man started to slow just enough that Cruz was able to come up on him from the left, and John from the right. John saw that it was definitely Jesus Perez. Before Perez could go any farther, John tackled him.

Perez fought but John had the man's wrists behind his back and cuffed him within seconds.

"I didn't do it," Perez said.

"Why do they always run when they're innocent?" John said to Cruz as he dragged Perez to his feet. To Perez, John said, "We've been looking for you. We've got a few questions."

Perez scowled. His nose was bleeding and he had road rash on one half of his face from being taken down in the street and landing facedown. "What do you want with me?"

"What don't we want to question you about?" John said dryly.

He jerked Perez along by his upper arm, marching him back to the house where the others waited. He brought Perez to a halt in front of Reese and Carter.

"The house is clean." Reese looked at Perez who smirked. "Why did you run? You must be guilty of something."

"Just hate cops," Perez said.

"Running is a surefire way to get you on Santa's naughty list." Reese and John escorted Perez to John's cruiser. Reese opened the back door and John pushed Perez's head down, forcing him to slide onto the seat. Reese shut the door firmly behind Perez.

A short time later, Perez was in an interrogation room, waiting. John, Reese, and Carter stood on one side of the one-way glass and looked at Perez.

"What are the chances that Perez murdered Carl Whitfield or had one of his men do it?" Reese said. "For all we know he could have had Freddy Victors murdered, too, and that's why we can't find him."

"It would no doubt be in retaliation for his brother and two of his men being murdered." Carter said. "I think that the working theory is right, that it was most likely Victors who killed Perez's men."

"Could be that Perez killed Whitfield and maybe Victors." John folded his arms and stared at Perez. "It's crossed my mind more than once."

"He's all yours," Reese said to John as he gestured toward the man sitting on the other side of the one-way glass. "Find out if that sonofabitch did it."

John entered the room. He reached the table, braced his palms on the surface, and leaned in close to Perez's face. "Did you kill Carl Whitfield or did you have one of your men do it for you?"

"No, but I'd like to shake the hand of the man who did." Perez grinned. "Or the woman, right? That kindergarten teacher who blew him away?"

John wanted to slam his fist into Perez's face, knocking the grin right off. But John kept his cool. Barely.

"Where's Freddy Victors?" John asked in a slow, measured tone.

"Hell if I know." Perez was still grinning. "Why don't you ask Carl Whitfield? Oh, yeah. He's dead. That pretty little bitch did it."

John's self control snapped. The rage that had been building inside him exploded outward and he lunged for Perez, grabbing him by his collar.

The door burst open and Reese charged into the room just as John was dragging Perez across the table toward him.

For a moment John saw Perez's terrified face, as if he were a mouse about to be ripped to shreds by a tiger.

Carter moved between Perez and John, forcing John to let go of Perez's shirt.

Reese held John back. "Not worth it, John." Reese nodded toward the open door. "Let us take care of this sniveling piece of garbage while you go take a breather."

Perez grinned.

Barely reining in his temper, John clenched his fists and stalked out of the room. He closed the door hard behind him.

"Don't let the bastard get to you," Cruz said as John walked into the room where they watched Reese and Carter interrogate Perez.

John said nothing, just watched with his eyes narrowed. Here they were with another worthless thug in the interrogation room and not getting a damned thing out of him. Yet another piece of garbage that was proving impossible to break.

When they were finished, Carter and Reese came out of the interrogation room. "He's hiding something," Reese said. "But I don't know if it's about Carl Whitfield's murder, Victors' disappearance, or something altogether different."

John nodded. Yeah, Perez was hiding something. But then Perez no doubt had a lot to hide.

Without saying anything else, John went to his desk and threw himself in his chair. He dragged his hand down his face. He had to find the bastard who killed Carl Whitfield, and he had to do it before he ran out of time.

Before Hollie ran out of time.

John's phone rang and he un-holstered it and checked the display screen. Garrett.

"Tell me you have something now," John said.

"I've tracked down the woman Freddy Victors has been sleeping with," Garrett said.

"How the hell did you find that out?" John shook his head. "We haven't come across one damned thing to indicate he has a girlfriend."

"Let's just say I have my ways." Garrett's tone was one of grim amusement.

"Ways that a cop can't use, no doubt." John leaned back in his chair. "What's her name?"

"Linda Solomon." Garrett gave John the woman's address and he typed it one-handed into a form on his computer. Linda lived in a much nicer part of town than where Freddy's trailer was located.

John gripped his phone more tightly. "Have you been in contact with her?"

"Just got the information and called it in to you," Garrett said.

"We'll get right on it and put her under surveillance," John said. "Thanks, Garrett. I owe you."

"You might regret that. I may need a favor sometime and I'll come knocking on your door."

"Anytime." John ended the call then arranged to have Linda Solomon put under surveillance.

Maybe now they'd get somewhere.

CHAPTER 13

*S*he runs through the forest as fast as she possibly can, her breath coming in harsh gasps. She'd never been a fast runner, but fear propels her forward.

Branches snag her hair, bushes scrape her arms, and she has to jump over fallen trees that slow her down. Her heart thunders and adrenaline surges through her so that she shakes like a junkie, yet it gives her the strength to go on. Adrenaline allows people to do things they normally couldn't do. Like run faster than the men following her.

I can't let them catch me. I can't!

Behind her the men crash through trees and bushes, the loud sounds growing closer and closer.

Her skin hot, her face flushed, she's certain her heart is going to explode.

"Bitch," one of them shouts. "Get back here." *His voice tells her he's closer now.* "I'm gonna teach you a lesson. Then I'm gonna kill you!"

Oh, God.

Fear drives her on, but still she can hear them gaining on her with every step she takes.

She trips on a tree root and screams as she topples forward. She lands hard on the ground, her face in dead leaves and pinecones. Her nose fills with the smell of pine and earth. Her hands claw at the soft damp earth as she struggles to push herself to her feet.

Before she can get up, one of the men grabs her by her hair and drags her backward. Pain shoots through her scalp and she screams as she looks into the cold dark eyes of a faceless man.

She screams again as she feels the cold metal of a gun barrel pressed to the back of her head.

Hollie bolted upright, a scream tearing from her throat. Her heart pounded and her entire body shook. Her body was coated with sweat.

"It's just a dream," came a soothing female voice and a light touch on her arm.

Hollie wildly looked around expecting to see forest but instead she saw a bedroom that was familiar yet not. She was in a king-sized bed, her fists clenching damp white sheets.

She met the kind gaze of a pretty woman who had dark hair cut short and warm hazel eyes. The woman was probably twenty-five years older than Hollie. She was sitting on the edge of the bed, her hand on Hollie's arm.

"You had a nightmare, Hollie," the woman said, her voice gentle and almost hypnotic. "Everything is all right."

But the moment the woman said that everything would be all right, it all came crashing down on Hollie at once. The living nightmare of the past couple of days was a reality far worse than her dream. She'd been in jail for forty-eight hours, accused of murdering her stepbrother, and was out on bail.

Tears flooded her eyes and rolled down her cheeks. She buried her face in her hands as the woman beside her continued to rub her back and murmur soothing words. She wasn't sure who the woman was, but she had a maternal way of calming Hollie down. She bit her lip lightly—it didn't hurt this time. How long had it been since Carl had hit her? She couldn't think clearly. More tears squeezed from her eyes as she thought of Carl, his murder being the reason she'd been in jail.

When Hollie gathered herself the best she could, she raised her head and looked at the woman who smiled and said, "I'm Angel, John's stepmother."

"Hi." Hollie sniffled as Angel handed her a tissue. "Where's John?"

"He had to go to work," Angel shifted on the bed and moved her hand away from Hollie's shoulder. "He didn't want you to wake up alone so he asked me to stay with you."

"Thank you for being here." Hollie dabbed at her nose with the tissue that was damp from her tears and Angel handed her another tissue. "How long was I asleep?"

Angel tilted her head to the side. "Almost twenty-four hours."

Hollie's eyes widened. "Twenty-four hours?"

Angel glanced at the clock beside John's bed. "It's almost noon and he brought you home around one yesterday afternoon. I'd say you needed the rest after all you've been through."

A sick sensation, like milk curdling in her belly, made Hollie feel like she was going to throw up. She swallowed back the awful feeling. "I guess so," she said.

"I washed your clothes." Angel gestured toward a chair beside the bureau, where Hollie's clothes were stacked. "We can go shopping for new clothes if you'd like. John doesn't think it's a good idea to go back to your ranch. Not yet."

"I think that would be great." Hollie looked at the clothes that she'd spent two days in. She really didn't want to wear them ever again, but for now it was a necessity.

Angel eased off the bed, getting to her feet. Hollie hadn't realized how tall Angel was until she stood. "Lunch is almost ready," Angel said. "Why don't you get dressed and join me in the kitchen?"

Despite feeling like she could never eat again, Hollie nodded. "I'll be right there."

After Angel left the room and had closed the door, Hollie slid out of bed, walked the short distance to the chair, and saw that her purse was sitting next to the clothing. She took off John's T-shirt and boxers. She wouldn't have minded staying in them—she had liked that connection between her and John.

Once she'd slipped into her own clean clothes, she went into the bathroom and looked into the mirror for a moment. Her gold-brown eyes were red, her eyes puffy, and she still had the remnants of a black eye. The split in her swollen lower lip was healing even though it still hurt a little.

She splashed cold water on her face. It helped liven her up a bit and her mind seemed a bit less foggy. She used John's comb to try to calm the sleep-tousled locks of her light brown hair. Her feet were cold so she tugged on her socks but didn't bother with shoes.

When she padded out of the room on the hardwood floor, she made her way toward the kitchen. She paused and looked at the fire dancing merrily in the fireplace before continuing to the kitchen. Had it only been a few days ago that she and John had spent time together at the table with mugs of hot chocolate?

The smell of chicken noodle soup and fresh cornbread made Hollie's stomach rumble. "Can I help with something?" she asked Angel as she entered the kitchen.

Angel nodded toward a cabinet as she took a large stockpot off of a red-hot burner, transferring it to a cool burner on the stove. "You can grab a couple of soup bowls from that cabinet and spoons from the drawer to the left of the sink."

While Hollie got out the bowls and spoons, Angel pulled a pan of cornbread from the oven and set the pan on a stone trivet. When Hollie set the bowls on the counter, Angel ladled soup with noodles into the bowls.

"Homemade noodles?" Hollie asked.

Angel nodded. "The cornbread is made from scratch, too." She nodded toward the fridge. "I have a casserole in there that we'll put in the oven to heat up when it's time for John to come home."

They ate in companionable silence. Hollie wasn't up to talking about anything that had happened, and was glad Angel didn't ask. After they finished eating and cleaning up what little mess there was, Hollie followed Angel into the living room.

Angel settled into the recliner and picked up a large hoop with a quilt stretched across it. She put a thimble on one finger and started hand quilting the material.

The quilt was pieced with material in vivid colors of blue, yellow, pink, purple, and green. "It's beautiful." Hollie sat on the sofa close to the recliner that Angel was sitting in. Hollie tucked her socked feet beneath her. "My mom used to quilt by hand. I still have one that she made when I was a little girl."

If Carl hadn't gotten hold of it—she hadn't noticed when she was cleaning up.

"I do some by hand and others on a quilting machine that's set up in my woman-cave at home," Angel said with a grin. "A glass of wine, new material, a pattern, and I'm ready to go."

Hollie laughed. It felt good to laugh. In that moment it was easy to forget all that was going on in her life. For a while they talked about John and Mike who were her stepsons, as well as Reese and Garrett who were her own children. She spoke with pride about each one of them.

"Sometimes they were all more trouble than they were worth," Angel said with a smile. "But they've got good hearts, every last one of them."

"They are fortunate to have you as their mother." Hollie spoke wistfully to Angel of her own mother.

When Hollie got to the part about her father remarrying so that she would have a mother, she went quiet and sagged a little as she thought of her stepmother and stepbrothers. Things could not have been more different between her family and John's.

Angel seemed to recognize the fact that Hollie needed a change of subject. "I think it's time to put that casserole in the oven."

She started to set aside the hoop but Hollie stood and said, "I'll do it. What temp and how long?"

Angel settled back in her seat and answered Hollie's questions. Hollie retreated to the kitchen and pre-heated the oven while she got out the casserole and put away the now dry dishes that had been stacked in the dish drainer.

After she put the casserole in the pre-heated oven, she returned to the living room and took her seat on the sofa, close to Angel.

"When John gets home, why don't I pick up a few things for you at the store?" Angel said. "Just give me your sizes and I'll see what I can find that will suit you."

"If it's not any trouble." Hollie gave Angel a grateful look. "To be honest, I'm afraid of running into people I know and my students. And then there are those who might recognize me from what they've read in newspapers or watched on TV. Not to mention reporters and photographers—the press is the last thing I want to see."

Angel nodded with understanding. "It's no trouble at all. I've been needing to pick up a few things for myself, so I'll kill two birds with one stone."

Hollie shuddered inwardly at the word "kill." She was glad that Angel didn't seem to notice.

Angel took a small pad of paper and a pencil from out of her quilting basket and handed both to Hollie who wrote down her sizes for shirts, jeans, panties, bra, and shoes, along with some toiletries. Holly wanted to burn what she was wearing now and she had no shampoo, conditioner, deodorant, and other things of her own—she'd had to use John's. When she was finished writing, she handed the notebook and pencil back to Angel and both items disappeared into the basket again.

The lock to the front door clicked and the dead bolt was shot back. For one moment, fear tore through Hollie. What if it was whoever had killed Carl? She didn't know why anyone would want to kill her, too, but the fear was still in her mind.

When the door opened, Hollie breathed a huge sigh of relief to see that it was John. Of course it was John. Who else could it have been?

She stood as John removed a black leather jacket from over his uniform. He gave each of them a tired smile as he draped the jacket over the arm of the sofa. He looked so good in his uniform, sexy and strong. He was a powerful man and his uniform emphasized that fact.

He walked across the room, and gave Hollie a big hug. As he hugged her, his stubbled jaw felt cool from having been outside and she shivered from the feel of his cold clothing through her warm T-shirt and jeans. When he released her from the hug he kissed her, a quick, firm kiss on her lips. Her lip only felt sore now and it didn't hurt when he kissed her. It surprised her that John would kiss her in front of his stepmother, considering they hadn't even been on a normal date.

"How are you holding up?" he asked Hollie as he held her.

"I'm fine." Hollie tried to smile back but knew that she hadn't been successful because of his worried expression.

He squeezed her to him again before releasing her. "Everything is going to be all right, Hollie. I'm going to make sure of it."

"Thank you." She looked at him and felt a deep confidence that this man would do everything in his power to prove her innocence. "I know you will."

Angel started putting her quilt, thimble, needle, and hoop into a large basket. "Now that you're home, John, there's no time like the present to get a little shopping done."

"Thanks, Mom." He gave her a hug when she got to her feet.

She kissed his cheek. "You know I'm here anytime you need me."

He smiled. "That goes both ways."

Angel gave Hollie a big hug next. "I'll bring some clothes by tomorrow morning. I'll leave the tags on so that you can return anything you don't want."

"Let me get you some cash out of my wallet—" Hollie's heart sank. Carl had taken what little cash she'd had out of her wallet the night he'd hit her. "I forgot, I don't have any. Can I write you a check?"

"We'll settle up later," Angel said. "I'm not worried about it in the least bit."

"Okay." Hollie managed a smile. "Thank you."

Angel started to pick up her quilting basket, but John held up his hand. "Let me get my jacket on and I'll carry it out to your car."

With a smile, Angel went to Hollie and hugged her tightly again. Angel grasped Hollie's upper arms as she drew away and held her gaze. "You hang in there. I know John will take care of this horrible mess you're in. I have no doubt about it."

"Thank you." Hollie couldn't help but feel better when Angel sounded so positive and sure that things were going to be okay.

Before leaving, Angel slid into her coat and pulled a woolen scarf around her neck as John put his own jacket on. Before John walked her out the front door, he picked up the basket then closed the door behind them. Hollie pulled aside the curtain draped overs the front window and watched John accompany Angel to her car.

When John looked over his shoulder, he saw Hollie looking out the window. For a long moment, for what seemed like an age, they held each other's gaze.

She wondered what he was thinking and wondered if he could read her mind. She could fall for this man so easily. And in truth, she was already falling for him.

CHAPTER 14

*J*ohn held Hollie's gaze as she looked at him through the window and it was like a punch to the gut. She looked so sweet and innocent. She didn't deserve any of what was happening to her.

Angel caught his attention by laying her hand on his arm and he tore his gaze from Hollie's to face Angel's again. "You were in such a hurry this morning that you didn't tell me anything about your relationship with Hollie." She paused. "Have you been dating long?"

John shook his head. "Just once." And that hadn't been a real date. He'd just let Hollie know that he wanted to get to know her better. He already felt like he'd known her for a very long time.

"So you're not involved?" Angel asked.

"If I have my way, we will be," he said.

She gave a slow nod. "I think she's a sweet girl. She'll be good for you."

"Yes, she will." His mouth tightened. "Whatever the case, I have to prove her innocence."

"You will." Angel reached up and kissed him on the cheek, her lips cold from the night's chill. "Now go on back in there and give that girl some company. She needs you."

And I need her, came the thought, but he didn't voice it aloud.

"I'll be over tomorrow with the clothes I'm going to pick up for her." Angel looked out into the early evening. "It's getting dark but the stores will be open for a while longer." She looked back at him. "Especially since Christmas is so close."

He nodded and opened the rear passenger door and set her basket on the seat before closing the door. He opened the driver's side door for her and closed it once she'd slid behind the wheel of her vehicle and started it. She buzzed down the window and waved toward the house. John looked over his shoulder and saw Hollie still standing there, still looking out the window, and she waved back.

"See you tomorrow, John," Angel said before she buzzed up her window. As she drove away, plumes of white came from the exhaust pipe, before disappearing in the chilly air.

He stood out in the cold, his hands shoved into his pockets and looked at several of his neighbors' glittering Christmas lights. He hadn't put up any himself. Hell, he hadn't even put up a Christmas tree. He spent the holidays with his family and had never had a reason to decorate his own place.

But with Hollie here... He'd like to make this Christmas special for her. Make it so that she had something positive and good in her life while it was being torn apart and turned upside down.

A thought kept pressing and pressing at his mind. He cared for Hollie in a way he'd never cared for a woman in his life. Maybe it was too soon to tell, maybe he was rushing things, maybe he was out of his godforsaken mind.

But he didn't care if he was rushing it. What he did care about was Hollie and seeing where things might take them. She could be the forever-woman he wasn't certain was real until now.

As he stood out in the cold, he pulled his cell phone out of his pocket and called Nadia.

She answered on the first ring. "What took you so long?"

Tension made John's muscles tight. There was no sense beating the bush about it. "We need to end this."

"What?" Nadia spoke in a shriek. "You can't dump me!"

"You're right. I can't dump you if we've never had that kind of relationship." He kept his tone low and even. "We agreed from the beginning that our arrangement was strictly friends with benefits."

"Things change," Nadia shouted. "What we have is good."

"We don't *have* anything." John's patience was waning. "I've cared for you as a friend and lover, but it didn't go any deeper in that."

"It's another woman, isn't it?" Nadia said the words savagely.

John gripped his phone tighter, feeling tension radiating throughout him. "What may or may not be happening in my personal life doesn't change anything. It's always been about sex and friendship. That's all."

"You can't do this to me," she wailed. "I won't let you."

"Nadia, this is it." He said the words firmly. "This is goodbye."

He disconnected the call and switched his phone to vibrate before he holstered it. He blew out his breath, which fogged in the cold night air. The phone vibrated in its holster but he ignored it.

It wasn't the way he'd wanted to end it, but Nadia had become possessive and demanding and he didn't see any other way of handling it. He felt like an ass. He had never intended to hurt her. He'd been stupid enough to believe that he could have that kind of a relationship with a woman.

Well, hell.

He turned and faced the house. Hollie was no longer in the window. Needing to see her more than anything, he started toward the front door.

Hollie felt both a thrill and a burst of nervousness as John walked through the door and locked it behind him. They were alone. In the same house. All night.

Cold air swirled into the warm house and she shivered as he removed his jacket.

When he'd set it aside, he walked toward her and she realized she needed another hug more than anything in the world at that moment. He seemed to read her mind because he wrapped her in his embrace the moment he reached her and held her for a long time.

When they finally drew apart, she looked up at him and smiled. "Thank you. I needed that."

He returned her smile. "Frankly, I did too."

She went willingly into his arms for another hug. She felt the stress, strain, and horrors of the past days fall away, if only for a moment. He didn't let her go when he raised his head and she looked up at him.

He brought his mouth down on hers in a slow, sensual kiss that rocked her to her toes. She wrapped her arms around his neck and pressed her body firmly against his. He gave a low groan as she felt him grow rigid against her belly and he moved apart from her, leaving his hands on her upper arms.

"I think maybe we should eat dinner." He looked like he was supremely uncomfortable and she wondered if it had anything to do with the tightness of his pants. "Something smells great."

Hollie breathed in the delicious smells too, and her mouth watered. "Angel made a pasta and cheese casserole." Hollie pulled her cell phone out of her pocket and glanced at the time. "It's almost ready to take out of the oven."

"I'm going to get out of this uniform and take a quick shower." He gave her a quick kiss on her forehead. "I'll be back in a few."

She smiled to herself and headed into the kitchen.

He returned fifteen minutes later, his hair damp from the shower. He wore a dark blue T-shirt and Wrangler jeans, his feet bare. He looked so damned sexy. When he moved toward her and kissed her on the top of her head, she caught his clean scent of soap and man and felt his body heat radiating from him.

Before going into the kitchen, he stoked the fire that had started to die.

Dinner was mostly quiet. She wanted to ask him about her case and yet she didn't want to. She was afraid of what he might have to say and she didn't want to ruin her night with him. For now she wanted to pretend that everything was okay, that she hadn't been booked for murder, and she just happened to be spending some time with a gorgeous hunk of a man.

"Leigh and Carilyn called me at the station today," he said after Hollie had taken a bite of casserole.

Hollie looked up at him.

"Your friends are worried about you and said you haven't been answering your phone," he continued.

Hollie chewed and swallowed. "I haven't felt up to talking to anyone." She took another forkful of casserole but didn't raise the fork. "My battery is low, too, and I don't have my charger." It had been off when she'd been in jail, so the battery hadn't died yet.

"You have the same cell phone that I do, so you can borrow my charger tonight." He studied her. "But that isn't the only reason why you haven't answered your phone."

She shook her head. "I'm too embarrassed."

He put his fingers over her free hand that was resting on the table and squeezed. "It's not your fault. You need to know people around you care for you."

"I'm afraid I'll see it in their eyes." Hollie suddenly didn't feel hungry anymore. "That question of whether or not I did it. I couldn't take seeing that."

John shook his head. "People who know you don't believe for a moment that you could have done this."

She stared at her plate for a long moment. "I keep seeing Carl in my mind." She looked up at John. "I see all that blood, hear him call to me, and see him die." A lump formed in her throat. "The images play in an endless loop in my mind." She didn't mention the nightmare. It hadn't been real. "I can't bring myself to be sorry that he's dead." She touched faded bruises on the side of her face.

"After what he put you through, I don't blame you one damn bit," John said. "I'd probably have come close to killing him for hurting you if I'd come across him before his murderer did."

Hollie didn't respond and John squeezed her fingers again.

When leftovers had been put away and dishes taken care of, they retreated to the living room. He offered her a choice between a bottle of Chardonnay and a six-pack of Blue Moon beer. When she told him she wasn't crazy about beer, he poured a glass of wine for her and grabbed a bottle of beer for himself.

They sat on the sofa, maybe six inches between them. She took a sip of her wine, and her hand shook a little as she set the glass on the coffee table. She felt suddenly nervous and didn't know what to do.

He set his beer bottle on the end table then reached for her and brought her close to him, just like the last time she was here and she'd cuddled with him on the couch. It felt so natural, so comfortable, as she snuggled into the curve of his arm and rested her head on his chest.

For a long time they stayed that way. His body felt so good against hers as he held her and it chased away the horrible reality that she had been living in. No, she wouldn't think about any of that for now.

She tilted her head back and he looked down at her. He'd never looked better than he did at that moment. His brown eyes were warm and caring, his expression tender in a way that she hadn't realized he was capable of.

He lowered his face to hers in a slow movement that made her almost crazy for him. She found herself holding her breath in anticipation. When his lips met hers, she sighed out her breath and let him take control of the kiss.

It was a slow but hungry kiss, like he was devouring her while savoring her taste. It was heady, her mind spinning with fire and longing and need.

She shifted in his arms, and before she knew what she was doing, she was in his lap, straddling him. She felt the hard ridge of his erection through his jeans and she squirmed against him.

He made a strangled sound and put his hands on her hips as if to stop her, but she grasped his hands in hers and placed them on her breasts. She tilted her head and arched her back, pressing her breasts close to him.

With a growl he pushed up her shirt and jerked down her bra so that her breasts jutted out. His mouth latched onto one of her nipples and she gasped as his tongue swirled over the taut nub.

"Yes," she whispered as she rubbed herself against him, as if riding him. "I need you." And she wanted to give her virginity to him, let him be the one who buried himself deep inside of her.

He squeezed her breasts as he licked and sucked her nipples. But then he moved his hands from her breasts to her hips and stopped her from moving.

"We can't do this." His voice was rough. "Not now."

She felt heat creep up her neck. "You don't want me."

"God, it's not that," he said, tension radiating through his body. "I want you more than I want to breathe. But now's not the right time. I'm not taking advantage of the vulnerable state you're in."

"It's not taking advantage of me if I want you." She moved her mouth close to his. "And I want you now."

CHAPTER 15

*H*ollie's mind whirled as she kissed John, and he returned her kiss with equal intensity. His taste, his scent, the feel of their bodies pressed together made her feel alive. She felt wanted, needed, cared for, and safe with him. It didn't matter that she hadn't known him that long. She'd known him from afar and he was everything she hoped for and more.

He caught her off guard when he took her by her waist and set her on the floor as he got to his feet. A dominant expression crossed his hard masculine features as he cradled her face in his hands and then he kissed her again.

When he raised his head, he took her by her hand and led her down the hallway to the master bedroom and the bed she'd slept in alone last night. His bed. Her heart beat faster as her socked feet padded on the wood floor and onto the rug beside his bed.

The entire time she'd been with him, she hadn't thought about what he might think of her body and her more than generous curves. For a moment she kept hearing the cruel words of her stepbrothers telling her she was fat. As John tugged her shirt over her head, she felt color rise to her face and she made a move to cover herself when the shirt was off.

He grasped her upper arms and pulled them away from her chest so that they were pinned by her sides. "Don't hide yourself from me." He moved his palms from her arms to her shoulders and back again. "Ever."

She nodded slowly as she realized he accepted her for who she was, flaws and all. "Okay," she said.

He gave her a heated smile as he reached behind her, unfastened her bra, and pushed the straps down her arms before dropping it to the floor. He cupped her heavy breasts in his hands, the soft flesh filling his palms as he lightly rubbed her nipples with his thumbs.

Her eyelids grew heavy with desire and she felt an ache between her thighs. She gripped his forearms, needing him to anchor her and keep her on her feet.

"I should have talked with you long before I did," he murmured as he caressed her breasts and nipples. "I've watched you from afar."

"I've always wanted to talk to you." She gave him a shy smile. "I've had a crush on you forever."

His mouth curved into a sexy grin. "A crush, huh?"

She felt a little embarrassed. "Maybe I shouldn't have said that."

He caressed the side of her face. "I'm glad you did. Maybe that's what it's been for me too, whenever I've seen you. A crush."

"You're just saying that." She smiled and pressed her bare breasts against his clothed chest, feeling the cotton of his T-shirt against her nipples.

"I don't say anything I don't mean." His words were firm yet filled with a sensuality that sent a shiver through her.

She slid her fingers into his hair and clenched the strands as she gave a soft moan. He caressed her back, moving his hands everywhere he possibly could before bringing them to the front of her jeans and unbuttoning them. Her belly flipped as he drew the zipper down, and then he was pushing her jeans over her hips and letting them drop to the floor. He knelt on one knee and tugged her black panties down, and she braced her hands on his shoulders as he removed each of her socks.

When he was finished and she was completely naked, he rose slowly to stand in front of her and pushed her hair over her shoulder in a sweet caress. "From the first moment I saw you, I thought you were one of the most beautiful women I'd ever seen." His voice was low and husky and gave her a thrill that traveled straight to her core. After everything that had been thrown at her over the years about her looks, his words surprised her. Yet after what he'd said earlier, she believed him.

How could this man who had seemed so unattainable actually feel this way about her? But then she'd only heard negative things about her body throughout her life after her father died. Maybe all those things her so-called family said to her, all those things they'd called her, weren't true.

No, they weren't true. She had value and John appreciated her for who she was.

He slid his fingers into her hair and brought her close to him so that her naked body was up against his clothed one. His jeans were rough against her belly and she could feel his erection through the tough cotton of his jeans.

She caught her breath as he moved his hand down her belly to the curls before slipping his finger into her wetness. She gave a moan as he touched the sensitive nub and it sent wild sensations straight to her abdomen.

His feet were bare but he still had his clothes on and she wanted him naked. Instead he surprised her by picking her up and carrying her to the bed. He moved the comforter with one hand and laid her on the soft sheets. Her heart beat faster as she looked into his warm brown eyes that held hers captive.

He eased onto the bed, pressing her legs apart with his palms on her knees, then knelt between her thighs. He lowered himself so that his hands were to either side of her shoulders before moving his mouth to hers and kissing her long and slow.

Without really thinking about it, she grasped his shoulders, digging her fingers into his T-shirt covered flesh. She was so wound up—she had to have release from the tight, needy sensations in her belly that connected to her sex. His kisses, his touches, were driving her desire to new heights.

He moved his mouth from hers, trailing his lips along her soft skin before reaching her breasts. She gasped as he teased her nipple, running his tongue in circles around the areola before sucking the taut nub. She clutched his shoulders even more tightly as he moved his mouth to her other nipple. He softly nipped at it and she gasped again before he slowly eased down her body until his broad shoulders pressed her thighs even wider.

"John." His name came out of her mouth in a hoarse whisper as he ran his tongue along the inside of one thigh before moving to the other without touching the part of her that needed it the most. She wanted to beg him but she bit her lip and held back the plea.

He raised his head just enough for her to see him close his eyes and inhale. "Your scent is driving me out of my mind." He opened his eyes and met her gaze before lowering his head and running his tongue along her folds.

A strangled cry rose up in her throat. She clenched her hands in the sheets and raised her hips without thinking about it. Her body seemed to move of its own accord as he stroked her folds and licked her clit. He slid two fingers inside her and pumped them as if he was taking her, his cock thrusting in and out.

Her mind spun as she felt her climax racing toward her. Her breaths came in short pants and she felt something coil low in her belly. It expanded and expanded, growing hotter and hotter throughout. She closed her eyes and could almost see the white-hot heat in her mind.

She knew she was about to lose it when her legs started to

vibrate. In the next moment, everything exploded like a super-nova in her mind and body. She cried out with the force of her orgasm, her body jerking and her hips twisting.

He made a low, hungry sound as he licked her a few more times. She shuddered before lying limp and relaxed on the bed. He rose up, moving over her again so that he was looking down at her, his eyes having gone from warm to fiery hot.

This time he kissed her hard with pent-up passion and a fierceness that rivaled a wild animal. His jeans abraded her skin as he pressed his erection against her mound and moved as though taking her.

He looked pained as he moved, his jaw tightening and a feral look in his eyes. He looked like he would take her hard and rough, and the thought made her squirm with a sense of need that only grew stronger and stronger with every moment that passed.

His throat worked. "I should stop now." It was almost as if he was telling himself. "It's too soon."

"Please don't wait." She grasped his biceps, feeling the strength and tenseness in him. She didn't care if she was begging anymore. "I need you now."

A rumble rose up from his chest and he eased off the bed. For a moment she thought he was stopping, but then he pulled his T-shirt over his head and tossed it onto her panties. A thrill went through her belly and she watched him unbutton his jeans before pushing them, along with his boxers, to the floor and stepping out of them.

He was magnificent naked, his body firm and muscular and completely void of any trace of fat. His cock—damn, it was so thick, long and hard that she knew he would fill her to the top.

Power radiated from him, not only from his body that echoed his profession, but in his desire. She knew without a doubt that he wanted to protect her from the fierceness reverberating through him, the instinct that would have him taking her as if he was an animal and she was his prey.

For a moment she felt suddenly nervous. It was supposed to hurt the first time you had sex and he was so big... Her throat worked. She wasn't going to be nervous. She refused to let anything ruin their time together.

He stepped closer to the bed. She thought of what it would be like to touch him...to feel his erection, to experience the power that radiated from him.

When he stood close to the bed, she turned onto her side, reached out and grasped his cock. He sucked in his breath as she moved her hand up and down the smooth, satiny length of him. She had never gone down on a man and she wondered what it would be like to have him in her mouth—what he might taste like, how it would feel.

Before she could try it, he drew away from her, opened the nightstand drawer, and grabbed a foil packet. Her cheeks warmed. She'd been so wrapped up in the idea of having him inside her that she hadn't thought about a condom.

He opened the packet and slowly rolled the condom down his cock. His gaze was hot as he watched her and she found the experience of watching him erotic. In the next moment he was moving onto the bed and kneeling between her thighs.

"I need to be deep inside you." He hooked his arms under her knees and moved her legs over his shoulders, pressing his cock against her folds. Her belly flipped and she tensed, waiting for the moment of penetration, the first time a man would take her. "I've never needed someone so much in my life," he said in a rough voice.

His words surprised her so much that for a moment she forgot he was going to be inside her.

He thrust hard inside her and she screamed. The pain tore through her and her eyes instantly watered and she bit her lip to keep from moaning.

"Hollie?" Shock registered on his features. "You're a virgin?"

She nodded, unable to say anything, trying to catch her breath.

"Why didn't you tell me?" He lowered her legs off of his shoulders and leaned down to kiss her tears away, first one then the other. "I would have taken it easier with you."

"It's okay." She smiled. "I like how you feel inside me." And she did. Despite the burning she loved how he filled her up.

He looked stunned and he wiped tears from her cheeks. "Are you sure you're all right?"

She nodded. "I'm fine."

"Damn, but I don't want to hurt you more," he said, his eyes dark with caring.

"I told you, I'm fine." She smiled. "I'm glad you're my first."

He looked concerned but moved in and out at a much slower pace. At first it hurt but then it began to feel better and better. Beyond better. It felt so good now that her lips parted and she gasped for air as she felt an orgasm rushing toward her.

"Are you all right?" He paused as he looked down at her with concern.

"Don't stop." She wriggled beneath his big, hard body. "It feels so good. Please don't stop."

He began moving in and out again, his thrusts becoming stronger as he watched her. She knew he was making sure she was all right.

She slipped her hands around him and found herself digging her nails into his back. "That feels so good. So, so good."

Her words seemed to relax him, letting him know that she was all right, and he increased his pace. Soon she felt no pain, no burn at all. What she felt was a pleasure so pure that she felt high with it. She moved her hips in time with his thrusts as he drove in and out of her.

A blinding light seared her mind, far more intense than her last orgasm. She screamed, the orgasm charging forward with a force that rocked her from head to toe. Her body shuddered as he continued to take her, throbbing with every stroke. She didn't know if she could take much more.

He shouted and arched his back, and she felt the force of his orgasm as his cock throbbed inside her. Her channel clenched him as she felt more spasms in her body, remnants of her incredible climax.

A droplet of sweat landed on her breast as he lowered his head and she saw his damp hair and the perspiration coating his face. He kissed her gently before sliding out of her and easing onto his side.

For a long moment he looked at her, stroking her hair from her face with his fingertips. His eyes held hers and she felt warm beneath his gaze.

"I'm sorry I hurt you," he said in a hoarse voice.

She smiled at him. "It was only for a moment. I'm glad it was you."

A look that seemed almost possessive came over his face and he crushed her against him. His arms were steel bands that held her naked body tightly against his, like he might never let her go.

Smiling, she snuggled against him. Even if it was temporary, she loved the feeling of being safe in his arms. She'd never felt safe like this and she welcomed it like she'd welcomed her now lover. She didn't know if this was going to be the first and only time, or if he would take her again and again.

She let out a little sigh. Whatever happened, she had tonight, and that was more than she could have asked for.

He cuddled her close, letting her rest her head on his shoulder as he put his hand on her hip and pulled her to him. He pressed his lips to her forehead. "Thank you for trusting me."

"I will always trust you," she said with a belief so firm she knew it couldn't be shaken. "Always."

"You're a special woman, Hollie." He smiled at her as he ran his finger down her nose to the tip.

"And you're a special man." She studied him and ran her finger along the line of his jaw and his eyes met hers for what seemed like forever. "Somehow I feel that I've known you forever. That I will always know you." *And love you*, went through her mind, startling her. It was too soon for love for either of them.

"I feel the same way." He squeezed her close to him. "I won't let anything happen to you, honey. I will always be here for you."

As he said the words she believed him, like she'd never believed anything before. Everything was going to be all right.

CHAPTER 16

*W*hen Hollie woke she blinked sleep from her eyes as she remembered where she was. She was in John's bed and she was alone. She sat up and brought the comforter over her breasts when she realized she was naked. A warm flush traveled through her body as she thought about what had happened last night with John.

It had been magic, sweeping her away with John to another place and time. It had been just the two of them in that special place where nothing bad ever happened. Only good.

Reality knocked at her consciousness. She looked out the window but couldn't tell how early it was because the sky was overcast. She glanced around the room and saw that the bedroom door was closed then spotted a clock on the nightstand to her right. It was just after ten. She never slept in like this as there were always chores to do and she was something of a morning person.

At the back of her mind was everything horrible that was happening in her life and she kept it shut away, not wanting to think about it right now. She'd always been a positive person despite the negativity clinging to her stepbrothers and their friends, especially Freddy. But right now her world seemed bleak and as gray as the overcast sky.

She climbed out of bed, feeling sore in a way she never had before. It was a good ache and it made her flush even more to think about how she'd gotten that way.

Naked, she headed into the bathroom, heated the shower, and stepped under the spray. With a sigh she tilted her head back, letting water run over her face and wetting her hair. Usually she took ten-minute showers but now she took her time, letting the warm water flow over her, washing away her cares for the moment.

After she finished showering, she dried off and put on a pair of John's boxers and a T-shirt. She loved the clean scent of the T-shirt and the feel of it covering her skin but hoped that Angel bought clothes and would have time to drop them off today.

When she opened the bedroom door, the warm smell of fresh-baked cookies washed over her. She headed into the living room and came to a complete stop.

A Christmas tree stood in front of the window, its colored lights blinking amongst the branches. It was a real blue spruce and it filled the room with a pungent but pleasing smell that reminded her of Christmases of long ago.

Shiny colored ornaments dangled from each branch, the balls reflecting the glow of the lights. She walked up to the tree, her gaze taking in its beauty. She touched a branch of the spruce, feeling its roughness between her fingers.

A fire crackled in the fireplace and she felt its warmth against her skin. Sprigs of holly decorated the mantel around the framed photographs. The room was filled with Christmas and it made her ache inside.

She hadn't celebrated Christmas or her birthday in years. Not since her mother had been killed in a car accident on that day and she was later left with a stepmother who couldn't stand her and stepbrothers who were mean, often cruel, to Hollie.

A lump rose in Hollie's throat and she fought back tears. This could be her last Christmas and birthday as a free woman if she was convicted of Carl's murder. She closed her eyes for a moment and breathed deeply before letting her breath out slowly. She repeated it until she'd calmed down and had pushed all negative thoughts away.

She opened her eyes and looked from the mantel to the spruce. She focused on the tree and smiled. John had done this, and it made all the difference.

"Good morning." John's low voice had her spinning to face him.

"Morning." She sounded breathless as she took him in from his dark hair to his deep brown eyes, and his clean-shaven jaws. His thumbs were hooked in his well-worn jeans and he wore a white T-shirt and broken-in brown western boots. "The Christmas decorations—it's all lovely," she said.

He gave her a sexy smile that had her belly swooping and sent tingles along her skin from the memories of last night. He moved toward her and caught her in his arms and kissed her. She breathed in his clean scent, tasted his unique flavor, and felt the heat of his body as he pressed himself against her.

"I hoped you would like it." He drew away. "I thought you needed some Christmas cheer."

"I love it." She returned his smile. "It's been a long, long time."

His brow furrowed. "You don't celebrate Christmas?"

She shook her head. "Not since my mother died in a car accident on Christmas Day." She let out her breath. "My father tried the next year, but neither one of us had the heart for it. Then my stepmother and brothers came into the picture and things were never the same."

"I'm sorry, honey." He brought her back into his arms. "We'll make new Christmas memories. All right?"

"Okay." The word came out uncertain at first and then stronger as she rested her head against his chest. "Okay."

He kissed her forehead. "Good."

She looked at the tree. "How did you find a Christmas tree so quickly?"

"I picked it up yesterday morning and put it in the backyard." He smiled. "Dug the Christmas decorations out of the garage."

"I like it." She studied the tree. "A lot."

"Are you hungry for lunch?" he asked. "I have the makings for sandwiches."

With a nod she faced him again. "Yes." He grasped her hand and she gripped his in return as she said, "Something smells wonderful."

"Sugar cookies." He gave her a quick grin.

"I love sugar cookies." The delicious smell made her mouth water as they entered the kitchen. About a dozen large cookies were on a cooling rack on the island. "Mmmm. Makes it feel even more like Christmas."

"You can have all the cookies you want, but sandwiches first, young lady," he said in a teasing tone as he released her hand and headed for the fridge.

He brought out lunchmeats, lettuce, tomato, onion, mustard, mayo, and whole grain bread. She took everything on hers as did he, and soon they were munching on their sandwiches. She had one to his three—apparently big man equaled big appetite.

"What's your favorite Christmas memory?" he asked her as they ate.

She thought about *Before*. Before the drunk driver and the accident that had claimed her mother's life.

"Every Christmas was a huge celebration." Hollie smiled. "Not only for the holiday, but because Christmas is also my birthday."

John raised his eyebrows. "With a name like Hollie I shouldn't be surprised your birthday is on Christmas Day."

She gave a nod. "Mom changed it from ending in a 'y' to an 'ie' to make it a little more unique."

"Seems like it might be tough having a birthday on such a big holiday," John said. "Did you get combination gifts?"

She shook her head. "There was always a pile of presents in traditional birthday giftwrap and another pile in Christmas wrapping paper. My mom and dad wanted to make sure my birthday wasn't forgotten in all the hustle and celebration of the holidays. My birthday cakes had colorful balloons or cartoon characters on them rather than poinsettias." She felt an ache in her throat. "That all ended when Mom died Christmas Day."

"I'm sorry, honey," John said, his eyes holding hers.

"It was a long time ago." She pushed her focus away from sad thoughts and then a smile touched her lips. "As for memories, I have a lot of good ones from those early years and I try to hold on to those." She tilted her head to the side as she thought about it as John ate his sandwich. "I can remember sitting up, waiting for Santa and watching the lights twinkle on the tree. Mom would bake gingerbread cookies and I would leave a plate out with a big glass of milk for Santa along with candied popcorn for the reindeer. All of it would be gone Christmas morning."

"Candied popcorn, huh?" John smiled. "I never knew reindeer liked the stuff."

"We would make nine balls and use red and green food coloring." She grinned. "Mom said Dasher, Dancer, Prancer, and Rudolph liked red and the other five reindeer preferred green. All nine balls would be gone because Santa took them to feed the reindeer. I was pretty darned excited every Christmas when I saw the empty plate, glass, and bowl."

John smiled. "Before Angel and my stepbrothers, our Christmases were pretty quiet. After they joined our family, let's say things got a little rowdier."

"How's that?" Hollie asked with amusement.

"We started out being darned competitive." John shook his head. "Dad and Angel had to give us the same gifts when we were younger to make things seem fair. One year we all got BB guns and tried to outshoot each other at target practice. When we were teenagers we were given rifles. We were all good at shooting but Mike was probably the best. It was damned close, though."

"Mike's the sheriff," Hollie said.

"He was always level-headed and the most straight and narrow of the four of us." John leaned back so that the chair was only resting on the back two legs. "As ornery as we all were, it's a wonder we each ended up in some branch of law enforcement."

After they finished lunch and tossed their paper plates, he handed her a round sugar cookie that had been sprinkled with red sugar.

"What, no tree or angel?" She gave a mock look of disapproval before taking a big bite of her cookie and making a sound of pleasure.

With a laugh, he took a cookie of his own and held it as he said, "There's an arts fair going on in Sedona tomorrow. Would you like to go? We can stay the night there."

"Can I leave town?" she asked with surprise.

He nodded. "As long as you don't leave the state, you're fine."

"I'd love to go." Her heart felt suddenly lighter. Getting out of the house and away from Prescott and her troubles sounded great and she found she was looking forward to the temporary escape. "When were you planning on leaving?"

"Around eight in the morning." He smiled. "Is that too early for you?"

She shook her head. "Not at all. I'll set my alarm so that I don't oversleep."

He looked like he was going to say something else when the doorbell rang. "Must be Angel," he said and gestured for Hollie to follow him.

She looked down at the T-shirt and boxers and her cheeks went warm. "I'm not dressed—"

He stopped, took her by the hand, and started leading her into the living room. "That's why Angel is here."

When they reached the door, John released Hollie's hand to open it. The door swung wide and Angel stood on the doorstep, her arms and hands filled with bags.

"You must have bought out the stores." John grinned as he took the bags from Angel and proceeded down the hall to his bedroom.

"How are you, sweetheart?" Angel gave Hollie a big hug.

"Great." Hollie offered Angel a smile as they drew apart. "We just had lunch." Angel slipped out of her jacket as Hollie glanced in the direction John had gone. "I think you went through more trouble than you should have, Angel."

"No trouble at all." Angel laid her jacket over the arm of the loveseat and gave Hollie a conspiratorial look. "Truth be told, I love to shop whether it's for myself or someone else."

Hollie grinned. "Shopping is one of my favorite pastimes, too. How much do I owe you?"

Angel gave a dismissive wave. "We'll figure that out once you have a chance to try everything on and we'll return whatever you don't like."

Hollie looked at Angel's trim figure. She was dressed in nice western pants, a western blouse, and dressy boots. "I'm sure that what you've picked out will be great," Hollie said, admiring how well put together Angel was.

Angel waved toward the hall that led to John's room. "Why don't you try everything on now?"

"Will do." Hollie started down the hall.

Angel said, "Come out and model the clothes."

Hollie glanced over her shoulder. "Okay."

She was surprised at how much Angel had purchased and spent the next forty-five minutes trying on the jeans, skirts, slacks, T-shirts, and blouses. Angel had also bought matching panties and bras for Hollie that fit just right. Only three things

HELD BY YOU

didn't look right or fit well and Angel said it was no problem at all to return them. Angel had bought Hollie the toiletries she'd asked for too.

When she'd put on the first outfit, she started down the hallway but stopped when she heard her name.

"I really like Hollie," Angel was saying. "There's indeed something special about her."

Holly felt her cheeks warm. She shouldn't be listening.

"I agree," John replied. "There is something special about her."

Hollie's belly flip-flopped.

"Do you have any leads in the case?" Angel asked.

John made a frustrated sound. "Not yet."

"Don't you worry," Angel said. "I've got a good feeling about everything. I think it will all turn out fine."

Hollie wished that she had a good feeling about it all, but she couldn't muster up anything but fear and worry.

She took a deep breath, raised her chin, and finished walking down the hall to the living room, where she modeled the first outfit.

After Hollie finished trying on clothes, she dressed in new light green panties and matching bra, and a pair of dark blue jeans along with a sea foam green top. She braided her hair and tugged on socks and soft leather shoes. When she finished dressing, she picked up the clothing she had changed into the night Carl was murdered and had worn in jail. She carried the lot to the kitchen and stuffed them into the garbage bag.

Angel was in the kitchen eating one of the soft sugar cookies as she and John talked. She glanced at Hollie when she threw away her clothes, but said nothing about it. When the clothes were ditched, Hollie found her purse on the sofa and dug out her checkbook. She had enough money for the clothes and incidentals, but not a lot more after bailing out her brothers. She still had the stash at the ranch and she was confident her stepbrothers would never find it.

Hollie wrote out a check to Angel who folded it and stuffed it in her jeans' pocket. "John told me you two are going to Sedona in the morning to the arts festival. You'll have a great time."

"I'm looking forward to it." Hollie smiled. She really was looking forward to getting away and spending time with John.

"I've got to go now." Angel gave Hollie a hug. "You two enjoy yourselves in Sedona." Angel moved to John who gave her a big bear hug.

Hollie watched Angel slip on her jacket and cold air swirled inside when John opened the door. Hollie shivered and gave Angel a little wave as she left the house with John walking her out to the car.

While John was outside with Angel, Hollie studied the Christmas tree. When was Christmas? She'd lost track of the days —everything seemed to be flying by so quickly.

The door opened, more cold air following John in before he closed it behind him. "You okay?" he asked as he walked toward her.

She realized she'd been frowning. She smiled at him. "I'm fine. I'm looking forward to going to Sedona tomorrow. It's been a while since I've been there."

After she put on a new jacket that Angel had purchased, Hollie and John spent the afternoon putting up Christmas lights outside, along with a wreath on the door and a large lighted snowman. Hollie's spirits rose as she spent time with John. He made her feel like everything was going to be okay. She just prayed it would be.

CHAPTER 17

"**W**hy don't I buy a couple bottles of water while you gas up?" Hollie grasped the handle to climb out of the passenger side of the truck. They were stopped at a gas station and convenience store on the way out of Prescott toward Sedona after stopping at an ATM so that Hollie could get some cash out of her account.

John pulled a ten from his wallet and held it out. "While you're getting the water, how about a package of trail mix?"

"I can pay for it," she said.

He shook his head. "I'm buying."

Reluctantly she took the ten. He'd already done so much for her, but she knew it wouldn't work to argue with him.

He reached her side of the truck and opened the door. Today he wore a brown Stetson and a cream western shirt along with Wranglers and brown boots. Whenever she had the chance she glanced at his ass. Damn, he was fine in those jeans. Although, he was pretty hot in his uniform too.

As he took her hand, warmth traveled through her body at the memories that came to her of last night. He'd made love to her again, even more intensely than he had the night before. He'd insisted on pleasuring her, taking his time, making her feel treasured every moment. They'd slept in each other's arms and she'd woken with her head against his chest and with him watching her closely.

She couldn't help the smile that curved the corner of her mouth at the memory.

After he helped her out of the truck and she'd grabbed her purse, he proceeded to gas up the truck as she headed toward the convenience store. She buttoned the dark blue blouse she wore when she noticed the button had escaped its hole, and then tucked the blouse into the flowing broomstick skirt that reached her ankles. She pulled the cell phone out of her purse and glanced at the screen to see that it was still early in the morning. It was ninety minutes from Prescott to Sedona and they'd wanted to reach the arts fair by ten. She shoved the phone back into her purse.

Hoping no one would recognize her as the "Killer Kindergarten Teacher," she ducked her head and went to the refrigerated cases that held sodas, energy drinks, and water. After she grabbed a couple of bottles of water, she went to the aisle with protein bars, jerky, and trail mix. She started to reach for a package of trail mix when a male voice jerked her out of her thoughts.

"Look who we have here," came Floyd's cold voice from behind her. "The bitch who killed Carl."

Hollie froze, a sick sensation weighing down her belly as her stepbrother closed in on her. "Heard you was out on bail."

"Why don't we beat the shit out of her?" Dickey spoke in a low, angry tone. "We'll take her out the back." He gave a nod toward the clerk who looked terrified. "Our 'friend' won't say a word when we do."

She straightened and turned to face her stepbrothers as she held the water bottles to her chest. "I didn't kill Carl."

"Now come on. We know you done it." Floyd's cold eyes were focused on her. "From what we hear, the cops have all the proof they need to put you in the pen."

Her stomach curdled but she tried not to show any weakness. "I didn't do it. I don't know who did."

Dickey's hand shot up and grabbed the strap of her purse. "Where's the money? Where's your stash?"

For a moment his abrupt change in subject caught her off guard and she almost lost hold of her purse. "I don't have a stash."

Floyd smirked as he poked something into her lower back—a gun, she realized with cold certainty. "We'll just go out the back door where our truck is. First you'll show us where the money is. Then we beat the shit out of you for killing our brother. Maybe even kill you."

She tilted her chin. "I'll scream."

Floyd pressed the gun harder into her side. "You do and I'll shoot you."

She swallowed. While John was gassing up his truck, she could be forced out the back door. He'd be waiting in his cab for her to return and would never know what happened to her. Maybe he'd see it on the security tapes, but she could be dead by the time he did.

How could she get away from Dickey and Floyd?

"Come on." Floyd nudged her with the gun. "Let's go."

He started to push her toward the back when everything that happened next came in a blur. John came up from behind Floyd and knocked the gun from his hand. It skittered across the convenience store's floor. Dickey took off toward the back.

Floyd gave a shout as John took him down, his knee on Floyd's lower back when he landed facedown on the floor. Two seconds flat and John had Floyd handcuffed, then he took a zip tie and bound Floyd's ankles.

John surged to his feet, retrieved Floyd's gun and put it into the waistband of his jeans, then put his hand on Hollie's arm.

"You okay?" She nodded. "Stay here and call 911," he said before he tore out the back of the convenience store after Dickey.

She took out her phone and started to dial the number for emergency when she heard sirens. She looked at the store clerk who had a scared look on his face.

"Did you call the police?" she called out to him.

He nodded. "I think that's them. The police station's not far."

Moments later, police cruisers pulled up to the store and officers charged into the store, guns drawn.

When an officer reached her, he aimed his gun at her chest and goose bumps prickled her arms. "Hands up," he said.

Déjà vu swept over Hollie as she raised her hands and looked down the barrel of the gun. She felt lightheaded and unsteady.

Another officer crouched beside Floyd. She saw that blood was flowing from his nose that must have broken when John took him down.

"What happened?" the officer asked as he looked up at Hollie.

"My stepbrothers—they tried to kidnap me and they were going to kill me." Her throat worked. "John stopped them." She looked down at Floyd. "John cuffed Floyd, but Dickey escaped."

"Who's John?" the officer asked.

"Lieutenant John McBride." Hands still in the air, she nodded toward the back. "He took off after Dickey."

The officer who'd had his gun trained on her lowered it. "Keep your hands where we can see them, Ms. Simmons."

It didn't surprise her that the officer recognized her. Carl's murder and her suspected involvement had been all over the news and likely every police officer knew it.

The other officer left through the back of the store, likely to give John backup. In moments, more police officers were on the scene.

She was made to sit on the floor, her back to the wall. She wondered if they wanted to cuff her and take her down to the station. What was taking John so long to return?

Finally, John came through the doorway that led to the back of the store. He spotted Hollie and went straight for her. He ignored the officers around him and took her by the hand. He brought her into his embrace and hugged her.

She gave a shuddering sob as the reality of her situation hit her with the force of a blow. Dickey and Floyd, who wanted to kill her, had almost kidnapped her. They had come so close to getting away with her.

"Thank you," she whispered to John as he held her.

Still holding her, he leaned back. "It's all right now." He brushed away a tear with his thumb.

"Where's Dickey?" she asked.

John frowned. "He got away."

A chill rolled down her spine.

"Don't worry." John gripped her tightly. "We'll get him."

She nodded, but a part of her didn't believe they would.

After John made sure she was all right, he gave his report to the officers and she gave her own account of all that her stepbrothers had done and said.

When all was finished and they were free to go, they walked out to John's truck. "Still up for going to Sedona?"

She blew out her breath. "More than ever."

THE RED ROCKS of Sedona gave Hollie a peaceful feeling as they drove into the town. She refused to dwell on what had happened a couple of hours ago. During the hour and a half drive from Prescott to Sedona, she'd had a chance to calm herself. She'd experienced worse, considering all that had happened leading up to the episode in the convenience store, starting with finding Carl's body to ending up in jail.

Yes, this little trip would be just what the doctor ordered.

John reached across the console for her hand and took it into his own. He gave her fingers a reassuring squeeze that sent warmth through her body. He gave her a quick smile when he glanced at her before looking back to the road.

Holiday decorations along the way to the arts festival added sparkle to the already beautiful area. So much time had passed since she'd last enjoyed the holidays. It was past time to pick up and start celebrating once again.

After all that had happened earlier, it was close to noon by the time they reached the arts fair, two hours after their intended arrival time. They had to park a good distance from the arts festival that was packed with people. After he helped her out of his truck, he gripped her hand as she walked at his side toward the display booths ahead. Every time he touched her, something fluttered in her belly and this time was no exception. She wondered if she'd ever get used to his touches and the way he made her feel.

He gripped her hand and she looked up at him. He was about eight inches taller than her five-five, so she had to tilt her head a bit to look up at him. His brown eyes held warmth and he didn't look as hard to her as he had before she started seeing him. She frowned to herself. If that's what this was—a relationship.

"What's wrong?" He studied her as they walked.

"Nothing." She gave him a bright smile. "Just excited to be here."

"You can't get past these cop instincts," John said. "You might as well get it out."

Her cheeks grew warm and she looked away from him. "Really, it's nothing."

He was watching her when she glanced back at him. "I want you to know that you can talk with me about anything. Anything at all."

She nodded. "I know." And she did...only she was too embarrassed to tell him about her thoughts regarding their relationship, whatever that might be.

He gripped her hand as they entered the maze of booths. Smells of Christmas were in the air, scents of pinecones and cinnamon teasing her nose. The first booth they came to had items created by local Native Americans. Hollie admired the pottery, dream catchers, woven blankets, and rugs.

"Do you have any Christmas shopping you need to do?" John asked as they visited the next booth that was filled with small sculptures made from scraps of metal, nuts, and bolts.

"Leigh and I usually exchange gifts," Hollie said. "I don't have anyone else."

"With a family the size of mine, we've gone to drawing names." John shook his head. "The whole clan gets together. At the rate our family is growing, though, I don't know if we can keep it up." He pushed his western hat up with his finger and she could see his eyes better. "This year I have Kelley, Reese's wife. Not sure what to get her."

"She's a detective, but feminine." Hollie considered it out loud. She gestured toward a leatherwork booth with belts, gun holsters, saddles, and other tooled leather items, many of them in smaller sizes for women. "How about a leather belt with a holster?"

"There's a thought." John gave a nod.

"Oh, and here they have puzzle boxes that can be used to hold jewelry." She nodded toward another booth with hand carved wooden boxes, animals and toys. The scent of cedar was strong as they neared the booth. "I might get Leigh one." Her gaze drifted toward a booth with gorgeous earrings made from glass, feathers, metal, and other materials. "Or I could get her a pair of earrings."

"Let's see what all's here and we can come back later," John said.

Hollie looked up ahead at other booths. "My thoughts, too."

They visited booths with beautiful silver and turquoise

jewelry; others with hand blown glass vases and ornaments; southwest paintings; porcelain and ceramic figurines; and numbered prints.

When they reached a booth with bronze sculptures, John smiled at the pretty petite blonde manning the booth. John put his arm around Hollie's waist in an almost possessive manner that sent a thrill through her belly.

"Hollie, this is my cousin Clint's wife, Ella." He turned to Ella. "This is Hollie Simmons." He gestured to the sculptures. "Ella is an artist and her work is displayed and sold in a Scottsdale art gallery."

Ella smiled and held out her hand. Hollie took it as Ella said, "A pleasure to meet you, Hollie."

"It's great to meet you, too." Hollie and Ella released hands and Hollie looked over the bronze sculptures in various sizes in the booth. "Is this all your work?"

"A good number of them are my smaller sculptures." Ella pushed her braid over her shoulder. "A friend of mine is an artist who has his work in a Prescott gallery and he's sculpted those bronzes." She nodded toward a grouping of bronze lions, bears, coiled rattlesnakes, eagles, elk, and wolves. She gestured to bronze rodeo-themed sculptures. "Those are mine."

Hollie went to Ella's display. Her sculptures were reminiscent of Remington's, only Ella's concentrated on rodeo cowboys and cowgirls. A bull rider, barrel racer, and rodeo clown were displayed among a sculpture of a cowboy roping a steer, one busting a bronc, and another hogtying a calf.

"They're gorgeous." Hollie saw the price tags and looked at Ella. "I wish I could afford one." With all the money she'd spent bailing out her brothers, she didn't have extra cash for much.

"I'm glad you like them." Ella's smile was engaging. "It's something I love to do."

"Like I love teaching." Hollie tried for a natural-looking smile.

She didn't want to dwell on what everyone might be thinking of her now.

Killer Kindergarten Teacher. She shuddered inwardly.

A couple walked up to the booth and Hollie stepped back. "We'll see you later, Ella," John said. Ella nodded and gave a little wave before turning her attention to the couple.

"I might buy one of Ella's small sculptures to give to Kelley." John looked thoughtful. "I think it's something she'd like."

They continued on through the fair, jostled by the crowd but enjoying it nonetheless. Hollie liked the feel of her hand in John's. It made her feel wanted and safe.

After visiting most of the booths, John left Hollie at the booth with the puzzle boxes while he bought one of Ella's small sculptures as a gift for Kelley. He returned with it in a box along with a bag containing other items that she assumed were for his stepmother and another family member.

During the time John had been gone, Hollie had selected a medium-sized jewelry puzzle box for Leigh and used the cash she'd taken out this morning to pay for it. She returned to the booth with silver and turquoise jewelry and picked out a pair of earrings made from Bisbee Blue turquoise for Angel as a thank you for all that she'd done for Hollie. When she made sure John wasn't close by or looking in her direction, she also bought a pocketknife inlaid with turquoise for him. The artist herself took care of Hollie and put the items in jewelry boxes. Hollie put the knife and earrings in the bag with the puzzle box.

While at the arts fair, Hollie had been able to forget about everything that had been happening to her and she'd thoroughly enjoyed her time with John.

As they walked away from the booth carrying their packages, the realities of her life tried to crash down on her, but she refused to let them.

John took her free hand in his and she gave him a smile. It felt so good walking at his side, as if everything would be okay, as if she didn't have any worries in the world.

A shrill voice shattered the moment. "How dare you!" A beautiful woman marched up to Hollie and John, swung her hand, and slapped John.

CHAPTER 18

*T*he gorgeous woman slapped John so hard his head turned to the side. She had a furious expression on her heart-shaped face while her vivid blue eyes sparked with fire. Her perfectly proportioned body was rigid with anger. Even angry she was beautiful.

A sickness settled in Hollie's belly as she watched the interaction, too stunned to think clearly as everything happened so fast.

John slowly turned to face the woman and she raised her hand, prepared to strike again. He let go of Hollie and snapped his arm up in time to catch the woman by her wrist before she could slap him a second time.

"Nadia." He said her name calmly as he held her wrist, but there was anger in his eyes. "This isn't the place or the time to have a discussion."

The nape of Hollie's neck prickled as she stared from John to the woman, whose face flushed with an expression that bordered on rage.

"How dare you?" the woman screeched as she jerked her wrist away from John's grip. "You think you can just fuck me and drop me?"

"Nadia, I've already discussed this with you." His tone was even but there was an edge to his voice. "It's over."

Nadia gave a scathing look as her gaze raked Hollie from head to toe. "Don't tell me this fat bitch is who you've been screwing around with."

Heat burned Hollie's face. Nadia's cruel words hurt like a punch to the gut.

John's expression hardened as he stared down Nadia. "You need to walk away."

Tingles erupted at the base of Hollie's skull. She knew she should walk away from this conversation, but she couldn't move.

"Please, John. Come back to me." Nadia suddenly turned to pleading. "What we had was good."

"There was never anything serious between us," he stated. "End of discussion."

Nadia's voice was so shrill this time that Hollie flinched. "You think you can treat me like dirt and get away with it?"

"We're going to leave now," John said firmly. "Goodbye, Nadia."

Hollie's legs still wouldn't move as every one of the woman's words echoed in her mind. John took Hollie by the hand, tugged her in the direction of the arts festival's parking lot, and her legs started to work again. She walked numbly at his side as Nadia continued to screech behind them. The words ceased to make sense at all.

Everything in her mind was jumbled. Her feelings of unworthiness were scrambled in her brain. Her brothers' cruel remarks and how they had always torn her down kept slamming into her brain. The fact that she was now called the "Killer Kindergarten Teacher" only made her feel even more unworthy. John was hard but handsome, stern yet kind. Why would he want to burden himself with her?

Nadia's shrieks suddenly cut off as Hollie and John reached his truck. He helped her into the passenger side. She wanted to shrug him off but let him open the door and boost her onto the running board and into her seat. She kept seeing the beautiful woman with her perfect body and features, and her flowing long blonde hair. Next to Nadia, Hollie felt frumpy, fat, and unattractive. How could John see anything in Hollie?

Once he'd come around to the driver's side and climbed in, he shut the door behind him. Without a word, he jabbed the keys into the ignition and pulled out of the parking lot. They rode in silence. Her mind was so full of doubt that she didn't even notice where he driving until he pulled out onto a lookout point with a view that would have been stunning if she wasn't feeling so sick inside.

He parked and shut off the engine and sat staring straight ahead. His silence only made her feel even worse. After a few moments, he climbed out of the truck, shut the door hard behind him, and came around to the passenger side. She didn't want to get out, but when he opened the door she ignored his hand and climbed down.

They walked to the ropes that kept sightseers from going any further. John hitched his hip against one post, his arms folded across his chest. Hollie looked away from him and stared at the view without really seeing it. A breeze teased her hair and blew it across her face. She pushed it away and tucked the strands behind her ears.

From her side vision she saw him rub the bridge of his nose with his thumb and forefinger before looking at her.

"When I told Nadia there was never anything serious between her and me, that was the truth," he finally said.

Hollie swallowed past the ache in her throat. "It's none of my business."

"I don't date in Prescott. Not until you, that is." He let out his breath. "I've seen women in Flagstaff and Sedona. Nadia lives here in the Sedona area, and I dated her off and on for the past six months. I broke it off recently."

Hollie could think of nothing to say.

"I've never dated seriously," John continued. "Not since Nancy Kennedy in high school." He gave a rueful expression. "That's an entirely different story, which obviously happened many years ago." He paused. "I've always treated women with respect, but I never found that special someone who I knew was worth the effort for forever."

Hollie's eyes burned. He didn't date seriously. What she had secretly wished for was vanishing in the wind. Then her thoughts turned to how messed up her life was, the fact that she wasn't beautiful like Nadia... She wouldn't blame him for not dating her for something more than casual.

John took her by the upper arms, turned her to face him, and forced her to look at him. "I didn't date anyone seriously because it was never right. Not until you."

Her stomach flip-flopped. What was he saying?

"You've changed everything." John gripped her upper arms more tightly. "Everything. You are the right one."

For one moment she wanted to throw her arms around him and let him hold her. His words were everything she could have hoped for.

No, it wasn't the right thing to do. She paused then shook her head. "I'm not the one for you." His forehead wrinkled and he frowned as she spoke. "With what's going on in my life, with how messed up everything is, we shouldn't be dating at all. I might be sent away for the rest of my life."

Frustration crossed his features. "I've told you that I'm going to save you, Hollie. You have got to trust me."

"There are no guarantees that you'll be able to." Words caught in her throat for a moment. "My life is royally screwed up right now. I'm screwed up. You don't need that."

A flash of anger in his eyes caught her off guard. "You are not screwed up. You've been stuck in a bad situation that isn't of your making and isn't your fault."

"I—it's not a good idea," she started.

He cut her off. "I told you that you have to trust me to save you, because I will. That's all there is to it." His grip still on her upper arms, he brought her roughly to him. "You are mine, Hollie. I will never let anything happen to you."

She gasped as he brought his mouth down hard on hers. He seemed to put everything into the kiss—anger, frustration, but power and dominance, too. It was as if he was making a statement, enforcing the fact that he thought she belonged to him.

He wouldn't break away from the kiss until she fell into it, giving herself up, surrendering to him. She returned his kiss with passion that matched his. Whatever happened, they had this moment, this time together, and that might have to be enough.

She was breathless when they broke apart and he took both her hands in his. "Come on. I've been planning on taking you out to dinner." He walked with her back to the truck and helped her into the passenger side. "There's a great little Mexican place just up the road."

"Sounds great." She gave him a smile before he closed the door behind her.

The restaurant wasn't far. It was a fifteen-minute wait to be seated, so they sat on a bench just inside the door and talked about the things they'd seen at the art fair. It was safe conversation and neither one of them brought up what had happened with Nadia. That subject was closed, at least for now. He also seemed to understand the need to not bring up anything stressful that was happening in her life right now—her brothers and the possibility of going to prison at the top of the list.

Twenty-minutes later they were seated and looking at the drink menu together. John ordered the house margarita while Hollie picked out the prickly pear margarita, before studying the dinner menus. Hollie decided on the beef burrito plate with rice and black beans while John went with an enchilada-style chimichanga, rice, and refried beans.

The server delivered the margaritas and Hollie's eyes widened at how huge they were. While they waited for their food, she sipped her margarita and felt herself loosen up and become more relaxed. "What was it like growing up in a houseful of boys?" she asked, figuring that was a safe topic.

John shook his head. "If you'd ask Angel, she'd probably say trouble. I mentioned before that we're all competitive, and that led to a little animosity at times. For the most part we got along, but sometimes it was Mike and I against Reese and Garrett. We'd side up and have ourselves a war."

"Didn't you all get along?" Hollie studied him. "I thought you did."

"When we weren't trying to outdo each other." The corner of John's mouth quirked. "I think we recognized that we're all good guys—that just didn't mean we got along all the time. No one was ever malicious or underhanded. We were just a bunch of boys hell-bent on getting into whatever trouble we could."

Hollie raised her eyebrows. "What kinds of things did you do?"

John shrugged. "Playing tricks, trying to outdo the others, attempting to get each other into trouble with Dad and Angel. All in all it was mostly harmless, but we gave Angel and Dad more than a few gray hairs."

"I was an only child when Mom died." Hollie didn't want to talk about what had happened after. "From what I've been told, I was a precocious child, but for the most part a good girl. My mom taught me to act like a lady from a young age."

"And you certainly are." John held her gaze. "A lady through and through."

Holly felt a blush redden her cheeks. "Thank you. That would make Mom happy to hear."

The Mexican restaurant was busy and it took some time before they were served. It was decorated for the holidays, adding to the festive feeling of the place. As they waited, they talked about their lives, Hollie always steering clear of the things that weren't good, and John didn't push her.

She felt a sense of pride as she talked to him about her kindergarteners and how they were doing with learning to write their names and the more complicated task of memorizing their phone numbers. They were learning to read simple stories and writing the alphabet. Because they were kindergarteners, it was more about the basics, but they were smart kids and most learned quickly. Arts and crafts projects were the most fun to do with the children.

"It's always fun to see what the kids come up with," Hollie said with a smile.

Dinner was excellent and the huge prickly pear margarita had given her a nice, mellow feeling. They took their time and it was late afternoon by the time they left the restaurant and headed to the resort. It seemed like forever since the incident with Nadia, as if it was a memory from long ago.

As they left the restaurant, John put his arm around her shoulders and she smiled at him before they walked out into the chilly day.

CHAPTER 19

The stunning views of the luxury resort stole Hollie's breath away. Tucked away in the forest, the resort was set at the doorway to the secluded Boynton Canyon, surrounded by red-rock canyons that inspired the mind and soul.

Once John and Hollie had registered at the resort's front desk, they went to their casita, John carrying the bags. The casita was lovely with rich earth colors and Native American décor. He set the bags on the king-sized bed, as she went to the sliding glass door that led to the patio. She stepped past the patio furniture and braced her hands on the railing, her lips parted as she took in the scenery.

John came up beside her and she tilted her chin to meet his gaze. "This is incredible." She looked back to the majestic scenery. "I can feel the energy here, yet a calm peacefulness too."

He braced his forearms on the patio enclosure and looked at all that surrounded them. "I thought you'd enjoy it."

She smiled. "I love it. Thank you for bringing me here. I'm going to be utterly spoiled after staying at this place."

He shifted so that he was standing closer to her. He slid his hand into her hair and cupped the back of her head. "You deserve to be pampered and spoiled." He lowered his head and captured her mouth with his.

She gave a soft sigh into his mouth and returned his kiss. Her mind felt like it was spinning, enhanced by the spiritual energy surrounding her. She gripped his biceps, clinging to him so that her knees wouldn't give out on her.

When he drew away from her, she felt almost naked from the loss of contact. He cupped her face in both of his hands. "You are a stunning woman, Hollie."

His words caught her off guard. He thought she was stunning?

He looked like he was going to say something else when his phone rang. He released her. "I've been waiting for a call from my stepbrother, Garrett, the PI. I hope you don't mind if I take this."

She smiled. "Of course not."

He withdrew his phone from the holster on his belt. When he looked at the screen, he said aloud. "It is Garrett." He pressed "answer" on the screen and brought the phone to his ear. "What do you have for me?"

He listened. "Good," he said after a long moment. "Let me know when you have more."

After he'd pressed "end", he tucked away the cell phone then turned to face Hollie. He grasped her around the waist and brought her firmly up against his rock-hard body. She felt his heat through her clothes, his erection against her belly. But more than that, she felt his possessiveness, his desire to make sure that she knew he was putting his stamp on her.

A delicious feeling ran through her body that made her skin feel as if liquid fire was sliding over her from head to toe.

In the next moment he was opening the sliding glass doors to the patio and taking her inside. "I'm going to show you just what you mean to me," he said. "I'm going to make love to you all night long. I don't intend to let you come up for air."

She caught her breath at his words that filled her with emotion and made her body tingle.

He kissed her while unbuttoning her blouse, as if not wanting to break their connection. She could sense the frustration in him as his big fingers worked to undo the buttons on her blouse. One by one he undid them before he pushed the blouse over her shoulders and down her arms.

The broomstick skirt was easier. All he had to do was drag it down over her hips and it fell to the floor around her ankles. Now only in black panties and a matching bra, she kicked off her flats and shoved the skirt away with her foot. He reached around her and unfastened her bra. She let the straps slide down her arms and dropped the bra. He pushed down her panties and she kicked them aside, next to the skirt.

He groaned as he brought her naked body up against him and his rough clothing chafed her body in the most erotic way. She wanted his clothes off and she began to unfasten his buttons. She needed his shirt off so badly that she fumbled in her hurry. Once the shirt was unbuttoned, he shrugged out of it and tossed it aside. She worked on his belt next before tackling the button of his jeans and dragging down the zipper.

With his hands on her shoulders, he toed off his boots and kicked them aside before removing his socks. She shoved his underwear down with his jeans at the same time she dropped to her knees and wrapped her fingers around his thick cock.

John went still as Hollie brought her mouth down on his erection. He'd planned on giving to her completely, not taking. But now that she was on her knees, his cock in her mouth, he found he could barely think, much less stop her and take over. It was as if she had taken control and he was at her mercy.

The feeling of her wet mouth around his cock made his gut tighten and he groaned. He watched her as she took him to the back of her throat and he sucked in his breath as she swirled her tongue along his cock.

Her name came out as a gravelly whisper. *"Hollie."*

She'd been a virgin when he'd taken her. How the hell had she learned to go down on a man like she was going down on him? The thought went through his mind that maybe she'd had oral sex with other men and a burst of hot jealousy tore through him.

He fisted his hands in her hair, showing her that she was his now. He wanted all of her—her heart, her mind, her body. No other man should ever enter her mind again because as far as he was concerned, there would be no other man but him.

Where had the jealous thoughts come from? How had he come to want her so much? To *need* her more than he needed water or air.

"I want to see your eyes." He barely got the words out and then clenched his teeth as she looked up at him.

She had the most beautiful honey-gold eyes. He brushed hair from her forehead with his fingertips as she looked at him with an innocence that caused his gut to twist.

In and out, her mouth so hot and wet, the feel of his cock at the back of her throat—it was all sending him out of his mind.

An orgasm hovered just seconds away. A part of him wanted to ask her if he could come in her mouth, but another part of him wanted to be inside her, to feel her naked body beneath his.

When he knew he was close to no return, he stilled her with his hands on her head. "Stop." He barely got the word out and drew his cock out of her mouth. "I don't want to come yet."

She looked up at him with such a sweet expression that he wanted to hold her close to him. He took her by her hands and brought her to her feet before wrapping her in his embrace. His cock was harder than he remembered it ever being as it pressed into her belly. She wrapped her arms around his neck and he lowered his head to kiss her, drinking in her scent and her taste.

When he raised his head, he held her face in his hands. "I've never wanted or needed anything or anyone like I need you,

Hollie. I will do anything for you. I will move mountains for you. Don't ever doubt me."

Her throat worked as she swallowed. Slowly she nodded. "I believe you."

"God, what you do to me." He groaned and kissed her again, loving the feeling of her naked body against his.

Her eyes widened when he scooped her into his arms and she held onto his neck as he carried her to the bed. He pulled the comforter back and laid her on the mattress, settling her head on a pillow.

He paused long enough to retrieve his jeans, pull his wallet out of a pocket, and slip a condom out. He tossed the packet onto the bed, close to her.

With his eyes focused on hers, he eased onto the bed and braced his hands on the bed to either side of her head as he looked down at her, drinking her up, feeling like he could never get enough of her body, her mind, her taste, her scent.

She looped her arms around his neck as he lowered his head and brought his mouth to hers. Primal instinct took over and he kissed her hard. A growl rose up in his throat, coming out of nowhere and he kissed her with even more passion.

Her passion matched his and the kiss became fierce, wild. He wanted to drive his cock inside her, taking her, staking his claim. He had to fight the instinct, the wildness inside him, and slid his lips to the corner of her mouth.

She whimpered and raised her hips, pressing her mound against his cock. He clenched his jaws, again having to fight the urge to drive inside her.

He licked and kissed her skin as he moved his lips along her shoulder, savoring the salty taste of her skin. He loved the little moans and gasps she made as he touched her. He sucked her nipples and she whimpered from the pleasure he was giving her.

"I'm going to show you how much you mean to me." The

words came out roughly. "I want you to feel it in the way I kiss you, feel it in the way I touch you."

He didn't care that they hadn't actually come together until recently. He was a man who knew what he wanted, a man who would do anything to get what he wanted. He was also a man who cared for and protected what was his.

Hollie was his. He would trade his life for hers.

"John." She sighed his name as he continued down from her breasts and dipped his tongue into her belly button. "I feel...I feel amazing with you."

"That's because you are amazing, honey," he said as he skimmed his lips lower yet.

Her skin was so soft against his callused hands and his mouth. He loved her full curves, the way her body felt beneath his. He wanted to cherish her, to let her know how he felt through the way he made love to her.

He settled his palms against the soft flesh of the insides of her thighs and pressed them wide before placing a kiss on her mound. He heard her catch her breath as he slid his tongue down and along her slit.

She gasped as he widened her folds with his fingers and he licked the length of her folds, from her clit and down to the soft skin just below. He slipped his palms under her ass and buried his face against her sweet flesh.

With a cry she tightened her fingers in his hair, pulling at the strands as she wriggled beneath him. He loved her taste, her scent, and liked the burn on his scalp as she pulled his hair and squirmed.

He licked her harder, and she made cries and whimpers that fueled his desire for her. He slid two fingers into her silken wet heat and moved them in and out as he sucked her clit. Her legs trembled to either side of his head she tensed and there was a charge in the air that told him she was close to coming.

She climaxed with a shout that gave him a feeling of intense satisfaction. He licked her until she stopped vibrating and her core stopped clenching around his fingers. Until her body relaxed as she came down from her orgasm high.

He couldn't wait any longer. He rose to his knees, tore open the foil packet, and rolled the condom down his cock as he held her gaze. Her eyes were heavy-lidded, her lips parted as she held her arms out to him. He positioned his cock at her entrance before kissing her and thrusting inside her, causing her to gasp.

It felt so damn good being inside her. He closed his eyes as he held still for a moment, feeling her tight core around his cock. He opened his eyes and began moving in and out, forcing himself to go slow. She gripped his shoulders as he rose. When he looked down at her he saw that her eyes had widened and her breath was coming in small pants.

His own breathing came harder, perspiration coating his skin. He tried to keep his pace slow but soon he couldn't hold back. He gritted his teeth and drove deeper. She wrapped her thighs around his hips and moved in time with his motions.

She grasped his shoulders tighter, her nails digging into his flesh. Her eyes glazed as if she was seeing something he couldn't before her back arched and she cried out his name, almost screaming as she came hard. Her body shuddered and she looked dizzy for a moment.

But even as her orgasm faded, she moved her hips in time with his, meeting his every thrust. He felt his mind start to spin. Sensation wound tight in his groin, expanding until it exploded inside him.

It was an orgasm like he'd never had before. He grew light-headed as he felt his climax from his scalp to his toes. He thrust a few times more, drawing out his orgasm until he couldn't take anymore of the sensation. Until he was completely spent.

His arms nearly felt weak as he stared down at her. A droplet of sweat rolled down the side of his face and landed on her collarbone. He kissed her hard before drawing her into his arms and holding her close.

"I'm never letting you go," he murmured. "Never."

She gave a little sigh and snuggled closer to him. "I feel safe with you," she said softly. "Like nothing could ever go wrong. As if nothing could ever hurt me."

He kissed her temple. "As long as I'm here, nothing ever will."

CHAPTER 20

*H*ollie smiled as she looked at the Christmas tree and its colorful lights and decorations. John had been so sweet to give her a Christmas while everything else in her life had gone to hell.

She refused to think of the negative right now, though. At times it seemed like it was something happening to someone else and she was the outsider watching as it unfolded.

John should be home soon. He'd gone to work early that morning and it was dark now. She had a casserole warming in the oven and the house smelled of cheese and pasta.

A thump came from the direction of the backdoor in the kitchen. Hollie frowned. It had been a loud thump, completely out of place. Had John come home? Was he coming in the back door instead of the front?

Another thump caused a chill to run down her spine and she turned to face the archway that led to the kitchen. Something wasn't right. She started to dig her phone out of her pocket when she heard a footstep and then she gasped.

Freddy Victors stepped into the kitchen doorway.

Blood drained from her face as he stepped closer to her, a leer on his face, somehow nastier than ever before.

She took a step back when Dickey appeared behind Freddy. His expression was dark, vicious.

Heart thumping, she whirled and ran for the front door. One of the men tackled her from behind, landing hard on her as he took her down to the floor. Something crashed to the floor as they hit an end table on the way down.

Breath whooshed from her lungs as her body hit the floor and her chin hit the tile too. Pain shot through her body and her face.

"I've got you now, slut," Freddy said in her ear, sending a shudder throughout her. "You're fucking that cop but I'm gonna show you what a real man's like." He scowled. "I'm so sick and tired of you and your kin fucking up my plans. I'm gonna have some real fun now."

Terror and adrenaline shot through her and using her forearms she tried to crawl from beneath Freddy. Shards of a broken ceramic lamp lay in front of her. She screamed as loud as she could in hopes that a neighbor might hear her.

Freddy grabbed her by her elbows and jerked her hands behind her back. He held her wrists in one of his hands and clamped his other hand over her mouth.

"Get out the duct tape." Freddy kept a tight hold on her as she struggled to get away from him.

Face still to the floor, she saw Dickey's boots as he approached. The next thing she knew he swung his leg back and drove his boot into her side once, then twice. "That's for killing Carl," he said in a menacing voice. "I'd kill you now if Freddy didn't want to fuck you first. Dunno what he'd want with a fat thing like you."

Pain screamed through her and her mind spun with it as he kicked her again and she cried out from behind Freddy's hand.

Dickey kicked her again and again. It was so excruciating that she was certain one or more of her ribs had cracked. Tears flooded her cheeks as the pain caused her body to seize.

"And that's for Floyd. He's in jail because of you, fat bitch." Dickey leaned close. "Yep. I'm gonna love killing you."

"Not 'til I've had my fun with her." Freddy's voice made her skin crawl. He moved his mouth close to her ear. "I told you I like broken things. Won't be long 'til you're broken so bad you'll be glad Dickey's gonna kill you."

A sob escaped her from behind Freddy's hand. Dickey knelt and she heard a tearing sound right before Freddy moved his hand and duct tape was slapped over her mouth. A moment more and her wrists were bound behind her with the tape.

Pain wracked her body and her skull as Freddy dragged her to her feet by her hair. More tears rushed down her cheeks. She didn't want to cry but the tears came of their own volition.

Was he going to rape her right here, right now? And then would Dickey kill her when Freddy finished?

A cell phone rang and Freddy pulled one out of his pocket. "What?" he snapped into the phone. "Two cops been asking about me? What did you tell 'em?" A long pause and then his face twisted with anger. "Don't fucking say anything else. Your place might be bugged." Another pause. "Shut the fuck up and don't call me again. I'll call you."

Freddy snapped his phone shut and stuffed it into his pocket. He pulled Hollie's hair as he turned his attention back to her. "Where were we, sugar?"

"We need to get her out of here before that cop comes home," Dickey said.

Freddy dragged her toward the back door. She stumbled and her arm brushed the Christmas tree, knocking off glass ornaments that shattered on the tile. Pieces of the ornaments crunched under Freddy's boots. He caught her by her upper arm before jerking her onward, taking her through the kitchen and out the back door, into the darkness.

Immediately she started shivering as the biting cold hit her. All she had on was a T-shirt, jeans, socks, and athletic shoes. Her shivering grew more violent as Freddy jerked her toward the front yard to a beat-up old car.

The only light in the street came from the Christmas light displays around the neighbors' yards. The two nearby streetlights must have been shot out or knocked out by well-aimed rocks. Still, she prayed a neighbor would see them.

When they reached the car, one of the men popped the trunk. They both lifted her and tossed her inside. Her head hit what felt like a tire and her vision wavered. She smelled oil and rubber. As she stared up at the men, her fear escalated.

A small spark of hope had her thinking that maybe she'd be able to loosen her hands and get her cell phone out of her pocket.

Freddy grabbed an old, dirty, and scratchy blanket from near her feet and threw it over her. "Can't have her dying of cold before we get a chance to use her."

The blanket wasn't much but it took a little of the chill off the top of her, not that it really mattered considering what they had planned for her. Beneath her the car was so cold that the blanket almost made no difference at all.

"Check her pockets," Freddy said. "Get rid of her cell phone if she has it on her."

The hope she'd held onto was sucked out of her as Dickey patted her down. He pulled the phone out of her front pocket before tossing it on the ground. It hit the ground with a clatter then she heard a crunch as one of the men clearly shattered the phone with his boot.

The warm tears leaking from her eyes felt like ice water as the air immediately chilled them.

Freddy grabbed the trunk lid and sneered as he looked down at her. "Hold on, sugar. We're taking you for a ride."

He slammed the trunk lid shut and she was left in darkness.

CHAPTER 21

*T*error caused Hollie's heart to jerk. All she could do now was pray that John would somehow find her, wherever it was that Freddy and Dickey were taking her.

The violent shivers continued through her body and she closed her eyes tight, trying to imagine the blanket was cocooning her whole body from the cold. The car started, its motor chugging as the motor revved. Tires pealed out beneath her as the car lurched forward.

A deep feeling of hopelessness clutched her insides. She was going to freeze to death or worse, Freddy was going to rape her before Dickey killed her.

She stared at the red taillight glowing in front of her face. As she looked at it, a thought came to her. What if she could kick out the one near her feet? Maybe a police officer would stop Floyd and Dickey for a missing taillight and she could make noise and catch the officer's attention. It was a long shot, but she had to try something.

She swung her leg, aiming for the taillight near her feet. Her foot missed and she stubbed her toe on the metal beside the light.

She winced from the pain in her chest and her toe but swung again. This time her foot connected with the light. It didn't budge but she wasn't about to give up. She kicked as hard as she could, over and over.

The taillight gave way and she pushed it partway out. She had to shift her body to shove the light all the way out with her foot. She didn't know how far the car had gone before she'd managed to kick out the light. If they were out of town, it wasn't going to do any good.

Just in case someone was driving behind her moving prison, she tried to stick her foot out the hole that was left now that the taillight was gone. It was no use. It was an older car with smaller lights and the hole on this vehicle was too small.

The longer the men drove, the more her hope faded. Kicking out the taillight had kept her mind off of the freezing cold but now she was more aware of it than ever. She was almost numb enough to not feel the aches and pains from being tackled and kicked in the side.

The car slowed and then the ride became jerky, jolting her as if they were going over rough terrain. Her eyes watered from the pain in her chest and side, caused by the bouncing car as it jerked her body around. Finally, the vehicle came to a hard stop and the engine was shut off.

She heard voices and then the trunk was popped open and Freddy and Dickey were looking down at her. They must have read the terror in her eyes because they both grinned. Together the men dragged her out of the car and dropped her on the ground. With her hands duct taped behind her back she had no way to break her fall. She hit the dirt and leaves hard.

From the smells of pine and rich earth, she realized she'd likely been driven into the forest. She sobbed from behind the tape. John would never find her out here.

Freddy and Dickey each grabbed one of her arms and pulled

her up to her feet and she saw Dickey's old truck to the left and a camper in front. A lone light shone in the camper, a glow spilling through a set of ragged curtains. She continued to shiver from the cold as they forced her forward.

When they reached the camper, Freddy jerked the door open. They forced her up two metal steps and into the camper. The inside was cramped, with not a lot of room to move around inside. Freddy shoved her again and she stumbled backward, her head hitting a cabinet. She saw the butt of a gun sticking out of his jacket pocket. A wild thought came to her mind. Maybe she could get hold of the gun—

Freddy pushed her again, this time toward the back where a bed was built into the camper. In the narrow aisle, they passed a tiny kitchen area with dirty dishes piled up in a sink next to a stovetop that had to be powered by propane. A cast iron frying pan and a cast iron Dutch oven were on the stove.

The mattress looked filthy, as did the blankets that were twisted and bunched up on it. When they reached the bed, Freddy backhanded her, twisting her around, and she fell. Again, unable to stop herself with her wrists taped, she landed facedown on the mattress that reeked with a sour smell and must. Pain raged through her chest from the cracked ribs.

"I want you to fight me, sugar." Floyd spoke from behind her as he cut the tape that bound her wrists. He rolled her onto her back, her arms free. "I like it when a woman tries to get away. Makes it a helluva lot more fun." He ripped the tape off her mouth. "I like to hear 'em scream, too."

It all seemed unreal as she stared up at Freddy, who had a self-satisfied leer on his face. Now she shuddered not from the cold but from the knowledge that Freddy was about to rape her.

Freddy shrugged out of his coat and tossed it behind him. She heard the thunk of the pistol she'd seen as the jacket hit the floor. "You wanna watch?" he said over his shoulder to Dickey.

"I'm gonna take a shit," Dickey said with a look of disgust.

Hollie was certain he wasn't disgusted because Freddy was going to rape her. It was the fact that Hollie was his stepsister. In some twisted way he thought it would be incestuous to get involved in the rape. "Tell me when you're done," Dickey said.

The door to the camper slammed shut behind Dickey as Freddy grabbed Hollie by her legs. With a look of lust, he dragged her closer to him. Panic sent her heart into overdrive and she kicked him and hit him with everything she had. Her body screamed with agony from the pain of her broken ribs as she struck out at him.

He grinned. "That's it, sugar. Fight me."

Tears flooded her eyes. The more she struggled, the more he laughed. He was so much stronger than her. He flicked the button of her jeans and jerked the zipper down. He yanked the jeans to her ankles, along with her panties.

Horror filled her as he leaned back to unbuckle his belt. She shoved herself back, trying to get to a sitting position, her jeans down to her shoes. He leered and unbuttoned his own jeans before pushing them down. His dick was erect, showing how aroused he was.

She glanced wildly around her, looking for something, anything, to hit him with. She spotted the cast iron pan and lunged for it.

Freddy's jeans were down to his knees as she wrapped her fingers around the handle of the pan. He saw her and reached out with one of his hands as he started to pull his jeans up from his knees with his other hand.

"Don't you dare, bitch or I'll hurt you bad." He yanked her by one ankle and she slid and almost dropped the pan. Anger twisted his features as he grabbed both her legs and started to pull her toward him.

She gripped the handle with both hands and swung the pan as hard as she could at Freddy's head.

The pan connected with his temple. He slumped and slid to

the floor.

Heart racing, terror ripping through her, she scrambled off the mattress, landing on Freddy's hand. He didn't move. She dropped the pan and jerked up her jeans, not taking the time to button or zip them and started to head for the door. She came to a stop—she would freeze outside before she could get far and die of exposure. She reached back and grabbed Freddy's jacket from where he had dropped it.

The pistol slid out of the pocket and thumped to the floor. She crouched down and grabbed it as Freddy groaned and stirred. When she wrapped her hand around the butt of the gun she raised it and pointed it at him.

Her hands shook as she gripped the gun. She aimed the gun at Freddy's head. She knew how to shoot and her finger was on the trigger. All she had to do was squeeze. That was all. Just squeeze the trigger.

She lowered the gun. She couldn't do it.

Despite the fact that Freddy had just about raped her and was going to let her stepbrother kill her, she couldn't get herself to shoot him. She'd never killed a man and she knew that it would somehow change her forever, in ways that could undo her.

No, she needed to get out of here before Dickey came back.

She stuffed the gun into the jacket pocket and turned to go to the door of the camper.

Freddy snatched one of her ankles.

She cried out as she fell to the floor, landing hard, almost blacking out from the pain in her chest. She rammed her other foot down on his head.

"Fuck!" he shouted and released her. "I'm gonna kill you, you fucking bitch!"

She surged to her feet and ran for the door. She glanced back. Freddy was caught up with his jeans around his ankles. She yanked the door open and stumbled down the two metal steps. They clattered and she was afraid that Dickey would hear. He could be coming toward the camper at any moment. She started to run into the forest then came to a stop. What if Dickey was in the direction she ran?

The panic mounting in her was accompanied by more adrenaline. What could she do?

Freddy would be coming out the door at any moment.

"You finished yet?" came Dickey's voice from behind the camper.

She started to run in the opposite direction but knew that between Freddy and Dickey, she wouldn't get very far.

Her gaze landed on the camper.

She dropped to her knees, flattened herself on the ground, and crawled beneath the camper. She had to bite her lip to keep from crying out from the pain in her body.

Dickey's footsteps came closer and she heard Freddy's footsteps thumping on the floor of the camper above her.

Freddy roared as he slammed open the door of the camper. "I'm gonna kill you!"

"What the fuck?" Dickey said.

Hollie didn't so much as breathe as she listened to Freddy and Dickey.

"She got away," Freddy said as he stepped to the ground. "The bitch got away."

"How the hell—?" Dickey started.

"Find her," Freddy shouted. "She couldn't have gotten far. Grab a flashlight and we'll get her."

She saw Dickey's boots as he raised a foot and took the two steps into the camper. The floor squeaked above her as she heard drawers slam.

"Got the flashlights," Dickey said as he opened the door and came down the steps. "Where's your jacket?"

"The bitch has it," Freddy said. "I don't have another one. We'll just have to find her."

"Let's go get her," Dickey's said.

She sagged on the ground while she watched the men's boots disappear as they hurried away from the camper.

CHAPTER 22

*J*ohn's breath hung in the air in a white fog as he left the police station. It was nearly dark and he was looking forward to getting home and seeing Hollie. He dug the keys to his truck out of his pocket as he headed across the parking lot. As he walked, his phone rang. He pulled the phone out of its holster and checked the display.

"Garrett," John said as he answered. "What's up?"

"Freddy Victors' girlfriend is back," Garrett said. "I'm sitting outside her home now. Thought you'd like to join me."

"Text me the address. I'll be right there." John pressed "end" and stuffed the phone back in its holster as he hurried to his truck. Within moments his phone chimed to tell him he had a message and he glanced at the screen and opened the message. Her home wasn't too far from the station.

John had put officers on surveillance on Linda Solomon's home, but had pulled them back when the discovered she was out of town.

Garrett had, however, tapped Linda's landline and had bugged her house while she'd been out of town, but so far they'd gotten nothing. They hadn't been able to track down a cell phone in her name so all they had was her landline. The tap and the bugs didn't do a damn bit of good since she hadn't been home.

The tap and bugs weren't legal but then Garrett was a PI and used unconventional methods when needed.

A sense of urgency had John driving over the speed limit until he reached Linda Solomon's neighborhood. He slowed down before pulling up his truck a couple of houses away from the woman's home and parking. It was almost dark now and Christmas lights glittered in front of some of the neighborhood homes.

As John strode toward Linda Solomon's house, Garrett walked toward him. As usual, he wore a western hat and shirt, jeans, and boots. His surveillance car was parked on the other side of the street facing in the opposite direction.

"When did she get back?" John asked Garrett when they met in front of the house.

They fell into step and headed up the sidewalk to the house. Garrett glanced at his watch. "Just over fifteen minutes ago—I called you as soon as she arrived. You made good time."

They climbed the porch steps to the door. While Garrett knocked, John stood to one side of the door to avoid being seen. He was in uniform and didn't want to scare off the woman. She might choose not to open the door with a police officer on her doorstep and no warrant.

A moment after Garrett knocked, the door opened just wide enough for the woman to look through.

"What do you want?" came a woman's voice, scratchy from years of smoking cigarettes.

"I want to talk with you about Freddy Victors," Garrett said.

"Why do you want to talk about Freddy?" The scowl in her voice was clear.

Garrett shrugged. "He's in some trouble. Maybe I can help."

"I don't know where he is." The woman sounded irritated. She started to close the door.

Garrett stuck his boot in the small space between the door and the frame. "Give me a couple of minutes." Garrett's voice was hard.

"Get your damned foot out of the way," she snarled.

John stepped into view. "A few words, ma'am."

Linda Solomon looked startled. He'd clearly thrown her off guard.

"What—?" She looked at Garrett then John. "What the hell is going on?"

"Where is Freddy, Linda?" John asked.

"I don't know." She said the words emphatically. "I've been visiting my sick mother. She lives in Flagstaff."

"Do you have any idea where he might be?" John asked. She shook her head and John kept his gaze on her, sizing her up. "It's in your best interest to let us know where he is. We need to question him in relation to a murder."

She narrowed her gaze. "Freddy wouldn't kill no one." She banged the door against Garrett's boot. "Get the hell off my porch."

Garrett moved his foot and Linda slammed the door shut. He looked at John. "Would you like to join me in the car for a moment?"

John gave a nod and they headed back down the stairs. It was dark now and Garrett had parked in the shadows, away from the streetlight. When they reached his car, John climbed into the passenger side while Garrett got into the driver's side.

Garrett switched on the listening device for the bugs he'd planted in the home.

"Freddy," came Linda's voice, captured by one of the bugs. She wasn't on the landline. "Two cops were here. They want to talk to you about a murder."

The phone call was one-sided. She had to be talking on a cell phone—a prepaid phone or someone else's phone not in her name.

A pause then, "I didn't tell them anything." Linda sounded irritated. "Where the hell are you? Up in that camper you said you have. Where is it? Groom Creek?"

Garrett and John looked at each other.

"You think bugs are planted in my house? I don't—" She snapped the words as she said, "Yeah, whatever." A beat later, "Fuck you."

They heard something slam and then banging around. Obviously she was pissed. Then came a sound like pots and pans clattering on the stove.

"Groom Creek," John said as he thought about the area and the most likely place where Freddy could be hiding in a camper in that area. It wasn't that far away.

"It's too dark to search now," John said. "I'll send out the alert and then tomorrow we can comb that area. Right now he's just wanted for questioning and isn't considered a suspect since the murder's been pinned on Hollie."

Garrett nodded. "I've got a guy who'll be here soon and can take over for me in case she says anything else. I need to get home to Ricki as soon as he gets here."

John clapped Garrett on the shoulder. "Thanks, bro."

Garrett gave him a nod. "We'll find the bastard and get Hollie off the hook."

"I intend to do exactly that," John said before climbing out of the car. He shut the door behind him and headed down the street to his truck. He stayed to the darkness the best he could as he passed her house on the opposite side of the street in case she was looking out the window.

Christmas lights glittered, some blinking on and off as he passed. One home had blow-up decorations including Disney characters and a mini Christmas merry-go-round. He wished he and Hollie were sharing a simple, carefree holiday. His insides warmed at the fact he was going home to her.

When John reached his truck, he climbed in, started the vehicle, and headed home.

Fifteen minutes later, John held his keys in one hand as he headed to the front door of his own house and he smiled. He'd been waiting all day to see Hollie. Thanks to Garrett, they'd now made some headway. John was certain that as soon as they found Freddy, they'd be able to prove he was the one who'd murdered Carl Whitfield.

Through the curtained window, John saw the Christmas tree's colorful lights winking. The cold air chilled his face but he barely noticed it. It would be good to be inside, warming up with Hollie in his arms.

The moment he stuck the key in the lock, he knew something was off. Call it cop-sense, call it intuition, call it a bad feeling crawling up the back of his spine... Whatever it was, he knew something was wrong.

With one hand hovering over his service weapon, he turned the key with his other and opened the door. "Hollie?" he called out.

Silence.

He stepped into the house and called out again. "Hollie?"

The house was warm and smelled of an over-baked casserole. The moment he stepped over the threshold, into the house, his heart started to pound against his breastbone. One of the living room lamps was smashed on the floor. Ornaments lay in shards near the tree.

Hollie!

His heart lurched and his skin crawled as he drew out his service weapon with one hand while pulling out his cell phone with his other. He called for backup before stuffing his phone back into its holster. He proceeded to hold his weapon in a two-handed grip as he checked every room for signs of Hollie.

Nothing. He found her purse sitting on an end table in the living room. Her jacket was hanging on a hook by the back door in the kitchen, not a good sign. It was too damned cold to be outside on a night like this without some kind of protection. Her phone was gone so he tried calling it but the call went straight to voicemail.

The wail of sirens sounded in the distance. In moments the sirens were cut and he heard vehicles coming to a stop outside the house, red and blue lights flashing through the curtains.

John opened the door and stepped onto the porch. One of the vehicles that had arrived was Reese's. He got out and started toward the house when he looked down. He frowned and gestured to John who met him on the sidewalk.

"You're sure Hollie's been kidnapped?" Reese asked with a grim expression.

"Positive." John gave a sharp nod. "There are signs of a struggle and her coat and purse are still in the house."

Reese nodded to the ground. "Can you tell if that's her cell phone?"

John's skin chilled and it had nothing to do with the weather. He crouched and looked at what remained of Hollie's phone. "Yeah, I believe it is."

Reese got out an evidence bag and a pulled on a latex glove before dropping the phone and its pieces into the bag. He straightened and looked at John. "Tell me everything."

Without going into detail about Garrett's phone tap on Linda Solomon's phone, John told Reese that Garrett had come up with a lead. They believed Freddy might be hiding out in a camper in Groom Creek. Reese knew his brother, Garrett, used unconventional methods to obtain information and that did not need to be discussed.

"Groom Creek?" Reese said. "Shit. It's not going to be easy tracking her down in that area, much less at night."

"We've got to find her." John felt like his head was going to explode. "The longer we wait, the greater the chance—" His throat closed off. He could barely hold in the fear or the rage that he felt at that moment. If anything happened to Hollie, he would hunt down Freddy Victors and kill him.

"We'll find her." Reese put his hand on John's shoulder. "Lock up and let's go."

Two officers set about going door-to-door to see if the neighbors had seen anything unusual, such as an unfamiliar vehicle or strangers to the neighborhood.

It wasn't long before John was on his way to Groom Creek with backup from the Prescott Police Department. Deputies from the sheriff's department were on their way, too.

John bit back the emotion cutting off his throat. He hadn't felt like this since he was a kid and his mother had passed away.

"Hold on, Hollie," he said aloud. "I'm coming."

CHAPTER 23

*H*ollie shuddered from the cold as her body pressed against the ground beneath the camper. Freddy's jacket helped, but it wasn't enough. If she didn't find help soon, she might fall victim to hypothermia.

But where could she go? Freddy and Dickey both had headed toward the highway, each taking either side of the road.

She stuck her hands in the pockets of Freddy's jacket to warm her hands and froze when her fingers met cold metal in both pockets. Freddy's pistol was in one pocket.

A set of keys was in the other pocket. Her heart lurched. Could one of the keys go to the car?

She waited until she couldn't see Freddy or Dickey anymore before she scrambled out from beneath the camper. She was injured and she was freezing cold. So very cold that she had a hard time moving as she stumbled toward the car.

When she reached the old, faded yellow car, she grabbed the ice-cold door handle and jerked the door open. She climbed inside, biting the inside of her cheek from the never-ending pain in her body. Her hands shook as she searched the key ring for the right key for the old car.

It was dark in the car but there was the light glow coming from the light shining through the camper windows. She raised the keys up to look at them in the dim light. The key ring was full and she had to sort through the keys. Her fingers trembled and she dropped the key ring. It clattered as it hit the floorboard.

She snatched them up again and glanced over her shoulder to see if either of the men was coming back to the camper. When she turned back she went through the keys. She found two that looked like they went to older vehicles. She jammed the first key into the ignition and to her relief it fit.

Heart beating like crazy, she started to put her foot on the brake pedal and discovered the car was a manual, not an automatic. She hadn't driven a manual since she was a teenager and even then she hadn't driven one more than a few times before the old truck had totally quit on them.

Damn, damn, damn!

She sorted through her memories. She needed to use the clutch and shift and—

Dear God, she wasn't entirely sure.

I can do this, she told herself. *I have to!* She put her hand on the gearshift. The interior wasn't well lit and she had a hard time telling where First and Reverse were.

She pressed in the clutch with her left foot and put her right on the accelerator as she turned the key in the ignition.

The car started on the second try. The gears ground when she put the car into what she thought was reverse. She was so terrified that she let out the clutch too quickly and the car lurched forward and stalled. Forward, not reverse.

She tried again, shifting so that she hoped she was now in reverse. This time she eased off the clutch. The car lurched backward but didn't stall.

With her stomach in knots, she backed up, the car jerking as she did. A crunch and a jolt and the car came to a sudden stop and died as she realized she'd just backed into a tree. If Dickey and Freddy hadn't heard her start the car, they likely had heard that.

She started the car and shifted again, this time into what she was pretty sure was first. Again the car lurched and jerked, the engine threatening to die. She stepped on the clutch then pressed the accelerator. The engine revved before she let out the clutch all the way.

As she started to drive away from the camper, she found herself staring into darkness. The headlights weren't on and forest was devoid of light, not even the moon was shining.

Panicked, she searched for a way to turn on the headlights. Relief went through her as she turned a knob and the lights came on.

She screamed when she saw Freddy and Dickey in the headlights.

The car stalled—in her hurry she'd let out the clutch too fast. The men ran toward her as she turned the key in the ignition and let out the clutch a little slower. The car leapt toward the men and they scattered to either side of the car as she pressed on the accelerator.

Her heart was beating so hard she felt as if it was going to leap out of her chest. She barely heard Freddy's and Dickey's shouts as they ran alongside the car and tried to reach for the door handles. She pressed harder on the accelerator and away from the men.

She drove the car out of the clearing and onto the rough road that had to lead to the highway. The road was narrow and jolted the car so that she bounced with every pothole it hit. She gritted her teeth as the rough ride caused pain to course through her chest.

The dirt road seemed to go on forever. The heater had come on when she started the car. At first it blew cold air, but soon the air began to warm up. Her fingers tingled as they started to thaw.

Lights appeared in her rearview mirror, the high beams

nearly blinding her. Freddy and Dickey were chasing her in Dickey's truck.

She was afraid to go faster—she could barely tell where the road was in her own headlights. But she had to get out of here.

The rear window shattered and she screamed. They were shooting at her.

She stomped on the accelerator. She was so terrified that she almost ceased to feel the pain in her body as the car jolted along the dirt road.

In front of her the road twisted around trees and bushes. She heard the sound of bullets hitting metal and knew she couldn't stop. If she did, they would kill her the moment they caught her.

Prickles ran over her body. Was that the highway ahead? Did her headlights just flash over asphalt?

Another shot from behind her. Her right front tire blew out.

She screamed as she lost control of the car. The engine revved as she hit the accelerator instead of the brake.

The car bucked off the dirt road. Metal crunched as the car slammed into a tree. There was no airbag in the old car to protect her and her head hit the steering wheel.

The world spun and then everything went black.

John drove like the devil was chasing him. His truck ate up the distance toward Groom Creek. It wasn't too far out of town, but it could be too late for Hollie if he didn't get there fast enough.

No. He refused to think that way. She was alive, damn it. He'd know if she wasn't. Wouldn't he?

As he drove, his phone rang and he saw that it was Reese. He answered it. "What do you have?"

"One of the neighbors saw a vehicle that he'd never seen in the neighborhood," Reese said. "The old guy said he thought it was a yellow 1970 Plymouth Duster. He was a mechanic for forty-five years before he retired and he owned one of those cars himself. He only saw the car."

"Mr. Rasmussen." John gripped the steering wheel. "He knows his vehicles. Anything else?"

"Nope," Reese said. "We're headed in your direction now."

The truck didn't move fast enough to suit John. He finally reached the Groom Creek area and he slowed. His gut twisted as he looked to either side of him. In the dark it was impossible to tell what road Freddy's camper might be on. They'd have to split up and check all of them.

John raised his cell phone to communicate with Garrett who drove directly behind him. John hit the speed dial number for his stepbrother.

Something to the side of the highway caught John's attention when it glinted in his headlights. He lowered the phone without responding to Garrett's voice as he answered the call.

John slammed on the brakes and came to a hard stop. He frowned and narrowed his gaze. His high beams had caught a glimpse of a car that had crashed into a tree. The hood was crumpled and the tree the car had hit was gouged and leaning as if it might fall to the forest floor.

That had to be the car that the neighbor said had been parked in front of John's house. He guided his truck to the side of the road. He'd barely parked when he grabbed a flashlight, jumped out of the truck, and jogged toward the car. The three police cars and Garrett's vehicle that had been following behind John's truck came to a stop.

Garrett was out of his vehicle almost as fast as John left his truck. John held his flashlight high in one fist, shining the light down on a faded yellow Plymouth car.

John's gut tightened as he hurried to the driver's side door that hung wide open. He shined the flashlight into the front seat. In the glow, John saw blood on the steering wheel. The keys were still in the ignition. He shined the light in the back seat and leaned over to check the floorboards in the back, too.

Garrett put his hand on the hood and met John's gaze. "Still warm."

John gave him a grim look. One of the officers handed John a pair of latex gloves and he pulled them on before taking the keys out of the ignition. He searched the key ring as he walked to the back of the car. Before he attempted to open the trunk, he noticed that one of the taillights was missing.

Heart pounding, John tried three keys and on the third try he popped open the trunk. He raised the lid and shined the light inside. His gaze took in the contents—a dirty old blanket and a flat spare tire along with garbage.

He looked at the missing taillight and frowned. It was smashed from the inside, as if someone had tried to kick it out.

Hollie.

He looked at the blanket again and in the glow of his flashlight he saw a long strand of hair that looked blonde or light brown. His stomach tightened. He raised the hair and dropped it into an evidence bag that an officer held out for him. He slid the keys into another evidence bag.

John aimed his light at the ground as he followed the trail that looked like heel marks in the soft soil. "Someone was dragged from the car." He followed the trail that ended a few feet away where a fresh set of tire tracks were. "And that someone was hauled into another vehicle. Looks like a truck with tires that have little tread left to them."

He followed the tire tracks and his heart sank when he saw that they ended at the highway. His gut told him that Hollie was in that truck.

Jaw set, he turned to face the officer who'd given him the gloves. "Head up the road and see what you can find."

John turned to stare at the dark highway as he took off the gloves with a snap and stuffed them in his jacket pocket.

"I'm coming for you, Hollie," he said beneath his breath. "I'm coming for you."

CHAPTER 24

*H*ollie moaned as she stirred. Pain split her head and her whole body hurt. She ached and every jolt sent shards of agony through her. Her thoughts were thick and heavy as she tried to think. Where was she? What had happened?

A chill rolled over her as the vehicle rattled along, and she blinked her eyes open. It was almost too dark to see but she realized that she was on the floorboard in the back of a club cab truck. She looked up and saw the gun rack above her with Dickey's rifles and shotgun.

She was still in Freddy's jacket and for the first time she noticed it reeked with the odors of chewing tobacco and sweat, but it kept her warm. The heater had to be on too, because her nose, fingers, and toes weren't numb from cold.

In the front seat she heard Freddy and Dickey bickering.

"Should've killed the bitch already," Dickey said.

"I want to make her suffer." Freddy's voice was dark and filled with malice. "I want to watch the light go out of her eyes."

She shuddered and started to gather Freddy's jacket more tightly around her but she couldn't. Her wrists were bound in front of her with duct tape, and her ankles were bound, too.

When she shifted she felt the weight of Freddy's gun in the pocket.

Her thoughts were coming more clearly now despite the ache in her head. She could tear the duct tape with her teeth. They hadn't put tape over her mouth this time.

No one ever said that Freddy and Dickey were sharpest knives in the drawer.

She brought her wrists to her mouth and started working on the duct tape with her teeth. The tape had only been wound around her wrists a couple of times but she still struggled to tear it a fraction at a time.

"Fuck." Freddy's voice caused Hollie to go still as the engine sputtered and the truck slowed. "We're out of gas."

"I've got five gallons in a can in the truck bed," Dickey said. "Pull over and I'll put it in the tank."

"You do that," Freddy said in a slow drawl that made a shiver travel up Hollie's spine.

The engine sputtered a few more times as the truck jolted off of the highway, rolled to a stop, and died. The passenger door opened letting in cold air and then the door slammed shut. She heard banging around in the bed of the truck and the clunk of metal against metal.

"That motherfucker is going to pay." Freddy turned in his seat and she saw him start to lean over the back of it.

She closed her eyes tightly and let the jacket fall over her wrists and the partially torn duct tape.

"Sugar, when you wake up you're going to wish you were dead. You can bet I'll take care of you," Freddy said.

She tried to keep her breathing slow and remained completely still. She heard a rattle above her and realized Freddy was taking one of the guns off of the gun rack. Goose bumps broke out on her skin and she was glad for the jacket covering her arms.

"But first I'm gonna take care of a problem, just like I did with Carl," Freddy said.

She bit the inside of her cheek as chills rolled through her. Freddy was going to shoot Dickey. Would he take her out now and shoot her too?

The driver's side door opened, letting more cold air in, and the truck groaned from the shift in weight. The door slammed shut.

Praying that Freddy wouldn't look in the back, she brought her wrists to her mouth again and worked even harder at the tape.

She heard the two men speaking but she couldn't tell what they were saying. She thought she heard Dickey begging Freddy for his life and then a loud crack sent more chills up her spine.

A moment later the driver's side door started to open and she hurried to lower her wrists beneath the jacket. Freddy whistled a tune as he shut the door and started the truck. The truck began to move again and bounced as he drove the truck from the side of the road and back onto the highway. She bit back a cry from the pain.

Freddy continued to whistle as she worked to tear through the tape with her teeth. He stopped whistling. "That sonofabitch, Jesus Perez, is gonna wish he was dead when I get through with him, too." Freddy's voice had gone hard, vicious. "After I fuck you and get rid of your ass, I'm gonna find that smug sonofabitch and blow off his face. I might've lost the fucking war but I'm not finished yet."

The duct tape finally gave way and Hollie let her breath out in a rush. She reached for her ankles, the tape easier to tear with her hands, and soon she was free.

The truck began to slow. She wrapped her hand around the cool grip of the pistol in the pocket of the jacket she was wearing. She drew it out, flicked off the safety, and raised it to point at the back of Freddy's head.

She pressed the barrel to Freddy's skull. "Pull over." Her voice was as ice-cold as the night.

Freddy stilled but then laughed, throwing her off guard. "You're not going to shoot me. You didn't when you had the chance in the camper. Besides, sugar, if you shoot me this truck's gonna end up in a ditch and it's all over."

"Try me." She cocked the gun, the click of metal loud in the truck cab. Her voice was cold, lacking emotion. "Ending up in a ditch and getting killed is better than getting raped and murdered by you."

Freddy laughed again as he looked at her in the rearview mirror and her eyes met his. "You ain't got the balls."

"No, I don't have balls," she said. "But I'm pissed off and that's good enough."

The truck suddenly swerved hard to the right. Hollie cried out as she lost her balance and fell sideways. Pain exploded in her chest as she hit the floorboard hard. The gun flew out of her grip and landed a good three feet away from her. The truck bounced and jolted, throwing her around.

The truck came to a hard stop nose downward. Her thoughts spun but she realized that Freddy had run them into a ditch after all. In the next moment he was leaning over the front seat. He yanked her by her hair as she scrambled for the gun.

"You've been fucking things up long enough." He jerked her backward, wrapped one hand around her throat, and put the barrel of a pistol to her head.

She screamed.

John dragged his hand down his face as he drove. What if Freddy had taken Hollie down any one of the roads into the forest?

He slammed his palm on the steering wheel as he drove down the dark highway. What the hell was he supposed to do? How was he going to find her?

"Give me a sign." John had never been religious but he found himself praying. "Tell me where to find her. Please, God, let her be all right."

His phone rang. He pulled it out of its holster and he glanced at the screen. Garrett. John glanced into his rearview mirror and saw that Garrett was no longer following him.

John frowned and answered the phone. "What's going on?"

"Spotted something on the side of the road and pulled over. It's Dickey Whitfield and he's dead. Shotgun to the chest. Body's still warm—he hasn't been dead long."

"Shit." John didn't stop driving. "If the body's still warm, Freddy's got to be just ahead."

"Yep," Garrett said. "Letting the boys and girls in blue take care of Dickey. I'm back on your tail."

"Got it." Prickles ran along John's forearms as he disconnected the call and stuffed the phone back in its holster on his belt.

Had that been the sign from God that he'd prayed for?

John pressed down on the accelerator, his speed climbing to seventy. It was a winding mountain road and his speed wasn't safe. He couldn't get himself to slow down.

If Freddy was still on the highway, John had to have a good chance of catching up with the bastard. John had a lead on Garrett, and as fast as John was driving, Garrett had yet to catch up with him.

Not more than fifteen minutes along, John saw a truck off the side of the road, nose in a ditch, headlights glowing eerily against dirt, rock, and dead grass. As John brought his truck to a hard stop, his truck fishtailed from a patch of ice on the road, but he corrected and pulled over just ahead of the old truck.

As he jumped out of his own truck, he recognized the vehicle as Dickey Whitfield's. Through the windows he saw two shadows and it looked like they were struggling.

John ran for the other vehicle as he pulled his Glock out of its holster. Holding the weapon in one hand, he started to yank the driver's side door open with his other.

The loud retort of a gun came from the truck cab as a bullet shattered the rear passenger's window and blood splattered the glass.

CHAPTER 25

*T*error for Hollie ripped through John as he held his gun in his hand as he yanked open the rear passenger door.

Hollie tumbled out.

John grabbed her body before she hit the ground. At the same time he caught her with one arm, he aimed his gun at Freddy who was slumped halfway over the driver's seat. Blood poured down the side of the man's neck.

"I shot him." Hollie's voice tore John's attention from the unconscious Freddy Victors to Hollie as he carried her one-armed out of harm's way. She sounded stunned as she said again, "I shot him."

"Are you okay, honey?" John's throat was thick with emotion as he continued to hold his gun on Freddy. "Did he shoot you?"

"I'm all right." She looked like she was in shock. "No, he didn't shoot me."

"Thank God." John held her gaze. "I love you, Hollie. I love you so damned much."

Her eyes widened and her lips parted. Before she could respond, a car pulled up behind the truck, came to a hard stop, and then parked. Garrett jumped out of the vehicle and ran toward John and Hollie.

John nodded toward Hollie. "Get her away while I take care of Victors."

Garrett helped Hollie as John held his service weapon and jerked open the driver's side door. Freddy didn't move.

After he checked to make sure Freddy wasn't holding a weapon, John dragged him out of the truck and laid him on the ground.

Freddy stirred and opened his glazed eyes. "Help me," he croaked.

Fury made John clench his Glock more tightly. The bastard had hurt Hollie and probably had intended to kill her. The last thing John wanted to do was save Freddy.

His jaw set, John tore the bottom half of Freddy's T-shirt off, made a compress with it, and pressed it to Freddy's neck. It looked like the bullet had nicked an artery. "Hold this and apply pressure."

John looked over his shoulder at Garrett and Hollie. She was pale in the light cast from Garrett's headlights. She had a laceration and a bump on her forehead and dried blood from the laceration was along the side of her face.

"Is she all right?" John's voice was hoarse as he asked Garrett the question.

"She'll be fine," Garrett said grimly.

Hollie nodded as she held her side and grimaced as if in pain. "I'm okay."

"I need something to keep this sonofabitch from bleeding out," John said. "I have a kit in my truck."

"I've got a first aid kit, too. I know where it is." Garrett got to his feet and headed to his car. In moments he returned with the kit. "Sure you want to save this scumbag?" Garrett's voice was hard and without compassion or pity.

"We need him to help prove Hollie's not guilty of murdering

her stepbrother," John said under his breath so that Freddy couldn't hear.

"It's too bad," Garrett muttered as he took over. "The world would be a better place without this sonofabitch."

John moved to Hollie and put one arm around her shoulders. At the same time, with his opposite hand, he made a call to report the situation, to tell his backup where they were, and requested two ambulances.

"Am I gonna die?" Freddy said, his chest rising and falling rapidly as he spoke.

"Unfortunately, I don't think so," Garrett said in a voice dark with anger and the promise of violence if provoked. "But that could change at any moment."

John tucked his phone into its holster. "Are you sure you're okay?" he asked Hollie as he held her in both of his arms.

"Yes." She pushed the word out on a gasp and let out a harsh breath. "I think a couple of my ribs are broken."

"Damn—" John had been about to let out something far worse, but he cut himself off as he relaxed his hold on her. "I'm so sorry, honey."

She sagged against him. "Thank God it's over." He heard her teeth chatter as she spoke.

John kissed the top of her head. "Let's get you into the truck where it's warm. You're freezing."

"Okay." She gasped as he helped her up.

Slowly they walked to the truck and she grimaced with every step. He helped her up and into the passenger seat while trying to keep from hurting her. He grabbed blankets from behind the front seat and tucked them around her.

He stood in front of her and placed his hand on her thigh, needing the contact with her. "I was so afraid I'd lost you." He cupped her face in his hands. "I don't know what I would have done if—"

"I'm here." She put her hands over his. "Everything is going to be all right."

He moved his mouth to hers, kissing her slowly, savoring her taste and her scent. He wanted to wrap her in his arms and hold her tight, but he couldn't, thanks to her injuries.

When he drew back he held her gaze with his. "I meant it when I said I love you. I've never felt anything like this, an emotion so strong it takes my breath away. God, I love you, Hollie."

"I love you too, John. More than words can say." She smiled at him. "Thank you for saving me."

He kissed her again before he asked, "Can you tell me what happened?"

She told him the story from the beginning, from the time she was kidnapped to escaping in the car and crashing into the tree. She went on to tell him about Freddy and Dickey taking her in the car and Freddy murdering Dickey. Her voice shook as she gave him the details of what had happened right before she shot Freddy.

"He had the gun to my head." Her throat worked as she swallowed. "I figured I didn't have anything to lose, so I pretended to pass out and slumped down. He dropped me and I grabbed the gun off the floorboard in the back." She shuddered as she continued. "Before he had time to react, I shot him. I'm lucky my dad taught me to shoot when I was young."

"You did great." John stroked hair from her eyes. "Not many people could have done what you did."

"Even though he was going to kill me, I don't know if I would have been able to live with myself if I killed him." She frowned. "That doesn't make sense, does it? I did aim to kill but he moved before I shot him."

"It makes perfect sense." John's throat was thick as he thought about how she had almost died. "You didn't want to be a murderer like he is."

189

"It feels like it would be a stain on my soul." She shook her head. "It's crazy."

"Everything's fine now." He squeezed both her knees. "You'll be proven innocent and Freddy's going to jail for a long, long time. We're pretty sure that Dickey isn't his only murder." John let out his breath. "You can bet he'll never hurt you again."

"Thank you." Her body seemed to sag more fully against the truck seat. "For everything."

"You don't need to thank me." John rubbed her upper arms. "You saved yourself. If you hadn't been so brave—I don't want to think of what could have happened."

The sounds of sirens met John's ears. Soon the cavalry would be here and he could get Hollie to a hospital.

Then he'd take her home with him, where she belonged.

In the days that followed, the police found evidence in Freddy's camper, including the shotgun that tied him to the murders of three members of Jesus Perez's gang. Freddy had killed Jesus' brother, Juan, along with one of Jesus' key men, Rudy Garcia, as well as Bobby Dominguez. He had, of course, also murdered Dickey Whitfield.

As part of a plea bargain to avoid the needle, Freddy admitted to killing Carl Whitfield, too, therefore vindicating Hollie. The night of the murder, Freddy had driven in the opposite direction Hollie had been going when she was headed to the ranch. He'd wanted to make sure he wouldn't be seen heading to town after he killed Carl.

Despite being cleared of all chargers, life had changed forever for Hollie. She didn't know that she could go back to her kindergarten class, much as she'd love to. Even though she was innocent, there was still a stain on her image from being dubbed the Killer Kindergarten Teacher. She knew that no one would look at her the same way again.

Her students were no doubt confused by what had happened, and maybe even a little afraid. Maybe they wouldn't be afraid of her, but they might be afraid because she could remind them of murder. She didn't want her students to have those worries or fears, or any other student in the future to deal with that ambiguity.

She spent the rest of the holidays before Christmas working through everything in her mind. What made the most sense? She loved working with children, loved teaching, and loved making the kids happy.

It was true that she had so much to think about, so much to consider. She just needed to make the right decision—right for her and right for her students.

For the time being she was staying with John, not wanting to go back to the ranch alone.

Floyd was in jail for attempted murder. Even though he was a horrible person, she couldn't help feeling bad for him, no matter how cruel he and his brothers had been to her. Floyd had lost a part of himself when his brothers had died, just like she'd lost a part of herself when her parents had each passed on.

To make sure they were safe, she did bring her stash of money and her treasured photo album to John's home. They'd gone through the pages of her photos together and she'd shared her memories with him. He'd dug out his own photo albums for older photos and shared newer digital photos on his iPad. She had few recent photos but treasured the ones she did have—a few with her students and several with her friends when they'd gone out together.

They talked like they had never talked before. She shared her concerns about going back into teaching, and he'd shared his longterm desire to retire from the police force and take up ranching.

Hollie had begun to heal from the injuries she'd sustained at

Freddy's and Dickey's hands. The emotional injuries wouldn't be as easy to heal.

Still, with John around, she couldn't help but feel a deep happiness in her heart and unconditional love. She loved John wholly and completely and couldn't imagine a day without him.

CHAPTER 26

Christmas morning, Hollie woke in John's bed to a soft kiss and the smells of pancakes, syrup, and coffee. She smiled up at John who gave her a sexy grin.

"Happy Birthday and Merry Christmas, honey." He nodded toward the tray in his hands. "Breakfast in bed for my princess."

"Merry Christmas to you, too." Delighting in the fact that John had been so thoughtful, she smiled. "And thank you."

She scooted up in bed, inwardly wincing a little from the remnants of pain in her ribs. John settled the breakfast tray over her lap. On one plate was a mound of pancakes with butter and syrup, and a smaller plate held several sausage links. Also on the tray were a tall glass of orange juice along with a hot mug of coffee with a small pitcher of creamer and a sugar jar.

He handed her a napkin that she placed on her lap. She insisted that he eat with her. He sat with her while he fed her the delicious pancakes and sausage links while taking a few bites himself.

When she was settled in to eat, John got up off the bed and drew back the curtains.

She caught her breath. "Snow!"

He grinned. "I ordered it to snow just for you."

She smiled as she looked out at the beautiful winter scene. "It's gorgeous. We'll have to go and play in it later."

With a nod he sat back on the bed, close to her. "Now eat up."

"I'm happy to do just that." Once she'd eaten all that she possibly could, John took the tray and set it aside on a trunk at the foot of the bed.

She started to get up but he said, "Stay right there."

He stood, went to the bureau, and opened the top drawer. He brought out a square box that was about three inches by three inches, wrapped in gold paper. He returned to the bed, sat on the edge of the mattress, and handed it to her. "Your birthday present."

She took the gold-wrapped gift and tore off the paper, revealing a chocolate brown velvet jeweler's box. She raised the lid and caught her breath.

Inside was a beautiful heart-shaped gold locket with an intricate design on its face. She looked at John. "It's gorgeous."

He smiled and nodded at the locket. "Open it."

From its velvet bed, she lifted the locket. She carefully opened the heart and her throat closed with emotion. On one side was a picture of her father, and on the other a picture of her mother.

"John!" She looked at him in amazement and tears stung the backs of her eyes. "It's beautiful." She closed the locket and held it to her chest. "I'll always have them close to me."

He brushed hair from her eyes. "I'm glad you like it."

"I more than like it." She flung her arms around his neck and held on. "I love it." She drew back and smiled at him. "But most of all I love you, John."

"I love you too, sweetheart." He took the locket from her. "Hold up your hair."

She obeyed and he clasped the locket around her neck. She looked down at the locket lying over her silky nightgown and resting between her breasts.

For a moment she wondered at how her life had changed. This Cinderella was finally free of her evil stepbrothers. Her Prince Charming had come to sweep her off her feet and had saved her in more than one way.

He took her by the hand. "Santa came, birthday girl. Let's see what he brought."

She laughed and climbed out of bed. She took a snuggly warm bathrobe off of a hook on the bathroom door and slipped into it before walking with John to the living room.

A small pile of presents wrapped in cheerful Christmas paper was under the tree. She sat beside the tree and John knelt next to her. He handed her a present wrapped in green paper with glittering red and white ornaments on it. The first gift was a pair of feather and turquoise earrings she'd admired at the Sedona arts festival.

He handed her a red-wrapped present. When she opened it, tears sprang to her eyes. It was a beautiful wooden music box inlaid with abalone and silver. "Thank you so much." She hugged him tightly. "It's gorgeous." The music box was different than the one that had been her grandmother's, which her stepbrother had broken, but just as beautiful. The fact that John gave it to her made it as special as her grandmother's had been to her. "You are an amazing man."

She opened the music box and smiled as it played a sweet tune, and she set the earrings he'd given her inside. She closed the lid and held the music box in her lap as she handed him a small oblong box wrapped in silver and gold paper.

He carefully tore off the paper, leaving him holding the simple brown box. He raised the lid and inside was the turquoise inlaid pocketknife she had picked out for him at the arts festival. He gave her a smile. "I love it." He planted a kiss on her forehead and hugged her.

When they finished unwrapping presents, Hollie took John's hand. "I want to talk with you about something."

He gave a nod. "All right."

"I'm not going back to the school when the next semester starts." She shook her head. "After everything that's happened, I think it's for the best." She felt a twinge of sadness, but she'd made up her mind.

He studied her. "I understand."

"I want to go into counseling and work with kids, especially special needs children," she said. "I double-majored in college, so I have a degree that makes me qualified to be a counselor."

He smiled and rested his arm around her shoulders. "You'll be great at it."

"You've talked about going into ranching after you leave the police force." She bit the inside of her lip before continuing. "What would you think about taking over my ranch and running it? The place needs some work but I've kept it up for the most part and all we'd have to do is buy some livestock and necessities to get it back up and running like it was when my dad was alive. We could work on a plan together."

John studied her. "I need to think on it, but truth be told, I know it's something I would enjoy doing with you at my side."

She felt a thrill go through her belly as he said the words. The fact that he wanted to do it at her side made her feel warm inside.

"Oh." He reached under the tree for a large box wrapped in paper with candy canes on it. "I almost forgot."

She took the box from him when he offered it to her. She glanced at him before tearing off the paper and opening the big box. When she looked inside, nestled in a bed of bubble wrap was a small red velvet box. Her lips parted as she picked up the small box and set the large box aside.

"Go ahead," he said. "Open it."

She slowly raised the lid and caught her breath. It was a diamond with tiny emeralds and rubies at two corners. They looked like tiny holly berries.

Heart pounding in her throat, she looked at John. He took the ring box from her and slipped out the ring.

"You are the woman I want to spend the rest of my life with," he said with a look in his eyes that told her of unfathomable love. "I can't imagine life without you." He grasped her left hand and raised it. "Will you marry me, Hollie?"

For a moment she was too stunned to move. It was so soon... but it felt like they'd already lived and loved a lifetime.

Tears bit at the backs of her eyes and she nodded. "Yes. Absolutely yes."

He slid the ring on her finger and she flung her arms around his neck and held onto him. When he drew back he wiped the tears from her cheeks with his thumbs. "You have just made me the happiest man in the world."

Her lips trembled as she smiled at him. "I love you, John. I can't wait to spend the rest of my life with you."

He cupped the back of her head and kissed her, the first of many in their new life together.

EXCERPT: BELONG TO YOU

CHAPTER 1

*A*nna Batista sat next to Chandra Johnson in the audience in the high school auditorium as they watched the debate between the two candidates for the office of Yavapai County Sheriff.

The incumbent, Sheriff Mike McBride, was facing off with his opponent, Chad Johnson. The debate between Sheriff McBride and Chad had been a heated one so far. Anna knew very little about the history between Mike and Chad, but she knew from Chandra that some bad blood between them went back a long way.

"Sheriff McBride, what is your opinion on the escalation of drugs and violence in Prescott and the county as a whole?" the moderator asked.

While Mike responded to the question, Anna cocked her head to the side and appraised him. She admired his strength and comfort under fire. He didn't act or talk like a politician and his down-to-earth demeanor and relaxed personality had made him popular, along with his sense of humor. One of the reasons she was certain he had been elected to county sheriff in the first place was his likability. He was tough but friendly, firm yet fair.

The fact that Mike was a dead-sexy cowboy was only the icing on the cake. All six-one of him was muscular, and his skin was deeply tanned from being out in the sun so often. His features were carved, his eyes a warm brown. Damn, but he was hot. The fact that he was in uniform didn't hurt at all.

Nice, she thought. *Very nice.*

A frown creased her face as she watched Chad Johnson take his turn at answering the same question about the escalation of drugs and violence in the area. Chad wore a business suit and bold red tie. He couldn't look more different than Mike.

"It's clear that something needs to be done in regard to this issue," Chad was saying. "Under my opponent's leadership, these problems have increased drastically."

Mike was given the opportunity for rebuttal and he laid out the statistics. Yes, there had been an escalation, but the number of arrests leading to conviction had also increased.

The moderator moved on to a question for Chad, asking what he thought the top priority should be for the next term for sheriff, other than public safety.

Chad gave one of his winning smiles and laid out his response. "Our children," he said. "Issues exist in the public school system and we need to make all the positive differences we can."

Anna mentally shook her head at Chad's canned answer to the question. He took the easy way out.

"Too bad Mike McBride is my brother's opponent." Chandra's platinum blonde hair swung forward as she leaned close to speak in Anna's ear. Anna caught the scent of Chandra's light floral perfume. "Mike is so gorgeous," Chandra said. "Beyond gorgeous." She sighed. "But he's the enemy."

Anna made a noncommittal response. How could she tell her friend that she thought Chad didn't stand a chance against Mike in the race or even in virility and looks?

With blond hair and blue eyes, Chad was good-looking and

popular in his own right, but he was all politician. He was an attorney in Prescott and his family owned a good portion of the town. The Johnsons, for the most part, were well known and respected, with just a couple of bad apples in the bunch.

Anna shifted in her seat as Chad made a couple of disparaging remarks about Mike's term in office. She hated it when politicians played dirty, and she was certain Chad was that kind of politician. So far the race hadn't been too bad, but she could see it coming.

After Anna and her family moved to Prescott, she'd become good friends with Chandra, who was genuine and kind.

On the other hand was her twin. Whenever Chad had spoken with Anna, it had always seemed to her that he was preparing to run for office. At the time she hadn't realized he would be running for sheriff.

She looked down at her fashionable chunky black heels as she crossed her legs then tugged down her red dress that reached low on her thighs. She linked her fingers and rested her hands on her bare knee. Even though Chad came off as having a pleasing personality, she knew it was something he had worked hard to cultivate. He had a politician's polish and presence, and Anna wondered how far that would take him.

Unlike Mike, who had been a decorated officer with the Prescott Police Department, Chad was an attorney with no law enforcement experience. However, in Arizona, having that kind of experience wasn't required. It was archaic. All that was necessary for the individual running was that he or she was a legal Arizona resident and resided in the county for which they wanted to be sheriff. That was it. No job application, background check, criminal history check, or psychological examination was required. After being elected, they weren't even given job evaluations like other county employees.

Anna mentally shook her head. The sheriff wielded a great deal of power in the county and was responsible for enforcing the law and running the county jails, along with a great deal of responsibility beyond. That included managing a budget in the millions. With respect to requirements for running for sheriff, Arizona was a bit of a backward state.

"What is your position on illegal immigration?" the moderator asked Chad.

Anna froze. Ice seemed to chill her spine as Chad looked directly at her. The eye contact only lasted a moment but it felt as if her heart had stopped. She felt Chandra stiffen beside her.

Chad continued speaking, but Anna could barely hear him because of the buzzing in her ears. She caught a few words including "tougher stand on illegal immigration," and "crack down on undocumented aliens in Yavapai County."

She had known the subject would come up. It was an important topic on both parties' platforms, and to the people. But having Chad look at her and meet her gaze caused a sickening sensation to twist her belly.

Does he know? She glanced at Chandra who was watching Chad. *Did Chandra tell him?* It seemed as though Chandra was making a point of focusing on Chad. She looked...angry. Had Chandra let something slip accidentally? She wasn't the kind of person to do that knowingly.

Anna was so wrapped up in her thoughts that she didn't hear Mike's response to the question on illegal immigration. She was just grateful he hadn't looked at her. Not that he had any reason to—she'd never even met the sheriff.

When the moderator moved on to a different topic, Anna tried to relax. She knew that with the way things were, she'd never be able to let her guard down. Ever. It just wasn't possible.

Chandra reached over and squeezed her hand. Anna met her gaze. Her friend said nothing, but her friendship and support were clear. If Chad had learned Anna's secret, then it either hadn't been through Chandra or it had been inadvertent.

Anna gave Chandra a little smile before she turned back to the debate that had finally ended.

"Come on," Chandra said. "I told Chad I'd meet him after the debate."

The last thing Anna wanted to do was face Chad, but she forced a smile. "Sure. Let's go."

Both candidates left the stage and Anna hooked her purse over her shoulder and followed Chandra backstage to see her brother. Anna lost Chandra as they wended their way through the crowded area and Anna stopped and frowned as she tried to look past shoulders. At five-one, Anna had a bit of a height disadvantage.

A man's tall form stopped right in front of her. She looked up and caught her breath. Mike McBride. Looking right at her.

His presence filled the room in a way that made her feel as if no one else was there but the two of them. His aura was far more commanding than she'd ever noticed with Chad. He had seemed larger than life on stage, and in person his personality was magnetic. She couldn't take her eyes off him.

Mike held out his hand. "I don't believe we've met. I'm Mike McBride."

She took his hand and stilled. The heat that traveled through her was like magic. It tingled through her as if she had the power now to cast a spell. She swallowed and spoke hesitantly, which was so unlike her. "I'm Anna. Anna Batista."

"A pleasure to meet you, Anna." He gave a sexy smile that melted her. The smile was nothing like what she'd seen from him before when he'd spoken to TV cameras or during the debate. It was as if this one was made just for her.

Then it hit her. What if he'd learned her secret? Was that why he was talking with her? To learn more?

"Nice to meet you, too." She managed to draw her hand away from his but couldn't seem to move away from him to go find Chandra.

"I saw you standing here," he said with ease. "You look a little lost."

His charm had her completely off balance. "I lost my friend in the crowd." She pushed long dark strands from her face. "I'm sure I'll find her, though." *All I have to do is find your opponent.*

"Can I help?" Mike asked.

Now that could be awkward. She shook her head. "I can find her."

Still smiling, he said, "I haven't seen you around before. If I had, I would have noticed."

He didn't seem anxious to let her go on her way. To tell the truth, she didn't want to. She found herself craving his nearness, wanting to get closer to him.

"This is my first debate." She smiled. "You were great up there."

"Thank you." His brown eyes studied her. "Are you from Prescott?"

She shook her head. "Not originally."

"Where did you come from before?" he asked.

She tried to remain casual. "The southern part of the state. Bisbee area."

"Nice place, Bisbee." He hooked his thumbs in his jeans' pockets. "Been a while since I've been. I usually stay at the Copper Queen Hotel."

"It is a great town and there's so much history." She probably sounded inane as she tried to think of something to say. "You're a Prescott native, aren't you?"

He gave a nod. "Born and raised."

It didn't surprise her that he wasn't trying to sell himself to her as a candidate. He had a confidence about him and genuine to the point that she couldn't imagine him putting on airs or lying, for that matter. No, definitely not a real politician. She knew in her heart that he ran for office because he cared about the county and its residents.

She found herself wanting to be closer to him, wanting to get to know him.

But that would be a bad idea. A real bad idea, and it had nothing to do with her best friend's brother being Mike's opponent.

Mike studied Anna and sized her up. She was beautiful and all of five-one if he guessed correctly, and he was usually right on the mark. Soft brown curls fell around her heart-shaped face past her shoulders and her perfume was intriguing, inviting. Her dark brown eyes were wide and had an innocent quality to them, yet a strength that told him she stood up for what she believed in. She might be petite but he'd bet she was a fireball beneath all the softness.

And damn but she drew him in, made him want to get closer to her.

At the same time he sensed she was holding back something… An emotion, a circumstance… Something was beneath that calm, beautiful surface. He had a keen ability to size up people and he had a feeling that there was more to Anna Batista than what met the eye.

It was the first time in a long time that he'd been so attracted to a woman that he wanted to get to know her better, to find out what made her tick.

"I'm headed out to get something to eat at the Hummingbird." He studied her dark eyes. "Would you like to join me?"

A surprised look flashed across her honey-brown features and her lips parted. For the briefest moment she hesitated. From her expression he thought she would say yes, but instead she looked apologetic and said, "I'm sorry but I can't."

He gave a slow nod and pulled a business card out of his shirt pocket and a pen from inside the leather jacket that he'd put on over his uniform. He wrote his number on the back and handed it to her with the handwritten side up. "If you'd like to get together sometime, here's my card. That's my personal cell number."

Again she looked like he'd caught her off-guard. "Okay." She took the card from him in her small fingers and tucked it into a purse that hung to her hip. "Have a nice dinner."

He smiled. "Perhaps another night, Anna." He liked the way her name tasted on his tongue as he said it. "I hope you'll give me a call."

"Thank you for inviting me." She smiled but he could see a hint of wariness in her eyes. "Good luck in the race."

Her response was a little disappointing. Maybe she'd have a change of heart and would give him a call.

"I'd best be going." He touched his fingers to the brim of his hat. "Have a good night."

"Good night," she said. Did she look a little disappointed?

He gave her a nod and a smile before heading toward the back way, his thoughts staying on the beautiful woman. His mind ached to turn and watch her as she moved through the crowd.

"Great job." Jack McBride slapped Mike on the back as he came up from behind. Mike stopped and Jack flashed a grin. "I'd say you kicked Johnson's ass."

Mike's cousin, Jack, was lean but all muscle and his features were angular. He had a perpetual five-o'clock shadow that gave him a tough, weathered look. He was a rancher like most of the McBrides were, and he had a nice spread with over one hundred fifty head of cattle.

"It was a good debate," Mike said. And it had been, despite the fact that Mike's opponent was a rival from his youth. Mike hooked his thumbs in his front pockets as he looked at his cousin. "Don't know about kicking his ass."

"You sure as hell did." Jack raised his western hat and pushed his hand through his dark hair before settling the hat back on his head. "Johnson doesn't belong in office. He doesn't know what the hell he's doing. You, on the other hand, are the best damn sheriff we've had as far back as I can remember."

With his thumbs in his pockets, Mike rocked back on his heels. "Are you going to be at John and Hollie's wedding?"

"Wouldn't miss it," Jack said with a nod. "Never thought I'd see John marry."

"Yeah, it's hard to believe he's tying the knot." Mike thought about his brother and the woman who captured his heart. "John found himself a good woman in Hollie."

"All of your brothers ended up with fine women," Jack said. "Can't say you'll see me settling down in a hurry."

Mike thought about his own confirmed bachelorhood, then thought of Anna. He shook his head. "I make it a policy to never say never."

Jack clapped his hand on Mike's shoulder. "I have a gut feeling you'll be next."

Mike's lips quirked into a smile. "I'm headed to the Hummingbird for a bite to eat. You up for dinner?"

"Hell, yes," Jack said. "As long as they've got plenty of their famous peach pie."

"I'll bet they do." Mike started once again toward the back door leading from the auditorium.

Jack fell into step beside him. "Then let's get the hell out of here."

Hair at Mike's nape prickled. It felt as if someone was watching him intently. He casually glanced over his shoulder and met Anna Batista's gaze. A pretty blush tinged her cheeks and she quickly looked away.

With a grin, Mike stepped into the night with his cousin. Just maybe he'd caught Anna's attention after all. He wasn't sure yet just how, but some way he *would* get to know the beautiful woman, and sooner rather than later.

CHAPTER 2

*A*nna's cheeks burned as she looked away from the gaze of the man who'd captured her attention so thoroughly. Mike McBride had just asked her out.

And she'd said no.

When Mike looked away and headed out the rear exit, Anna covertly watched his retreating form. His shoulders were broad, his ass and athletic thighs so very fine. His Stetson only added to his sexiness.

She swallowed, disappointment making her stomach feel heavy. She'd wanted to say yes so badly. The fact that he was her best friend's brother's enemy had kept her from accepting his invitation to dinner—she couldn't get into a relationship with the sheriff and not upset her friend. Chandra was so close to her twin brother.

Of course Mike had only asked Anna out to eat, so what was she worried about? That didn't mean he was interested in dating her.

But she'd seen it in his eyes. He'd pretty much made it clear he was interested. Why else would he ask her? It certainly couldn't be for her vote—a politician didn't take an average citizen out just to get her vote.

A thought came to her. Why shouldn't she go out with Mike? Maybe she could meet him for drinks. Yes, she'd call him and tell him she'd have a drink or two with him.

Mind made up, she straightened her bearing and looked once again for Chandra.

"Anna." A man's voice had her whirling around. *Chad.*

"Hi, Chad." She gave him a smile but had a hard time putting warmth behind it. "Good debate." Feeling nervous, she looked over her shoulder. "Where's Chandra?"

"She's talking with one of my aides." Chad gave Anna a practiced smile. "I saw you with my opponent. McBride gave you his card."

Something in his eyes told her that what he was going to say next wasn't good. "Yes." She gave him a bright smile. "You politicians like to score points with your voters."

He didn't blink. "McBride wrote his number on the back of his card."

"How do you know that?" she asked before she could stop herself.

"Speculation." Chad studied her. "You just confirmed it."

Her cheeks felt warm. "Like I said, politicians—"

He cut her off. "Don't play it down, Anna. I could see he's interested in you."

Her skin tingled, but this time it was from irritation. "What do you want, Chad?"

He gave her a politician's smile. "Just making sure I haven't lost you to the other side."

"Of course not." She looked past Chad and spotted Chandra. "I've got to meet up with your sister. See you."

Chad gave a smile and a nod. But somehow she felt like clammy fingers crawled along her spine. He had to know her secret and he was just playing with her, waiting for the right time to talk with her about it.

She waved at Chandra, catching her friend's attention. Without a backward glance at Chad, Anna worked her way toward Chandra who had just finished talking with a young man, who must have been one of the aides that Chad had mentioned. Chandra started toward Anna and they met up halfway.

"Where have you been?" Chandra asked. "You disappeared."

"Lost you in the crowd." Anna shrugged. "Got waylaid and then escaped and made it here."

With a laugh, Chandra said, "By who?"

Anna felt a moment's discomfort. "Your brother for one. He made it clear he wants my vote."

Chandra laughed. "That's my brother."

"Chandra," A female voice interrupted and Anna turned and saw that it was Leigh Monroe. Leigh caught sight of Anna and said as she reached them, "Hi, Anna."

"Haven't seen you around for a while," Anna said. "What's up?"

Leigh hesitated.

"Leigh broke up with her boyfriend again not long after I broke up with Neal," Chandra said. "They split before last Christmas, got together again, then just broke up a few days ago."

Anna reached out and touched Leigh's arm. "I'm sorry."

"It's all good." Leigh's throat worked and it looked as if she wanted nothing better than to change the subject. "We—we're just friends now."

"Leigh and I are going to Jo-Jo's to check out the guys," Chandra said. "Want to join us?"

Anna had the feeling that Leigh and Chandra were going to be talking more about the men who had broken their hearts recently than checking out the men, and she didn't want to interrupt. She also thought about her decision to call Mike. He was the only man she wanted to check out right now.

"I'll take a rain check," Anna said. "Where are you parked?" she asked Chandra.

"Out back." Chandra pointed toward the rear exit.

"I'm in front of the auditorium." Anna jerked her thumb in that direction and took a couple of steps back as she spoke. "I'll call you." To Leigh she added, "See you later, Leigh."

The two women waved and Anna waved back before heading out into the auditorium. As she walked, she pulled her cell phone out of her purse along with Mike's business card, and then punched his number into her phone. After another deep breath, she raised the phone to her ear.

A beat later, Mike's deep voice came on the line. "Sheriff McBride."

"Hi, Sheriff." Anna swallowed as butterflies batted around in her belly. "This is Anna Batista. We just met."

"Hi, Anna." He had a smile in his voice. "Taking me up on dinner?"

"Why don't we have a drink?" She would play it cool. "I can meet you at Nectars."

"That would be fine," he said. "What time?"

She gripped her phone tightly. "How about eight?"

"Perfect," he said. "I'll see you then, Anna."

"See you," she said before she disconnected the call.

Her hand gripped the strap of her purse until it ached. When she walked down the steps from the stage to the auditorium, she saw that the auditorium was mostly deserted now. She hurried up an aisle and out the front entrance.

Now she had two hours to kill and she had no idea what to do with the time. She settled on going shopping. It was a Wednesday and still early enough that plenty of stores would still be open.

The air was cool when she stepped out through the double doors. Fortunately she'd had a good parking place, so she reached her Honda in no time. She unlocked the car and grabbed a sweater from the backseat and slipped it on.

After she got into her car, she called her aunt to tell her she wouldn't be home for dinner then started the vehicle. Which store should she start off with? She decided to check out the sales at her favorite dress boutique. She put her car into gear and headed to the store.

Right now she was feeling unsettled. The feeling likely had something to do with Chad looking right at her when he was talking about illegal immigration.

Shopping was a comfort and would get her mind off of the subject. Like some people ate or smoked for comfort, she shopped. She had a closet full of shoes and stylish clothing. She usually bought things on sale—she was a smart shopper—but she probably spent more than she should.

Okay, truth was that she did buy more than she should, but she only bought what she could afford.

She had a great reputation as an event planner and was paid well. She worked not only in Prescott and Flagstaff, but traveled to parts of the Phoenix metro area. Her work frequently took her out of town, but she didn't mind the travel and she loved planning and executing the events. Weddings were her bread and butter, but birthdays, parties, conventions, and trade shows also brought in a good income.

Her favorite boutique was open like she'd thought and she found a parking spot directly in front of it. Devora Snow was dressing a mannequin as Anna walked into the store. Bells jangled as she entered.

"Anna." Devora smiled. Blue and purple streaks of color in her dark blonde hair glimmered in the shop's lighting. "What are you up to?"

"Hi, Dev." Anna returned the smile. "I'm here to check your sale rack, of course."

"Of course." Devora flashed a grin as she moved away from the mannequin to the sale rack. "And I have just the dress for you. It's your size and a petite."

In moments Anna was trying on a stunning black dress that hugged her curves and rose high on her thighs. She came out of the changing room to model the dress for Devora.

"Beautiful." Devora clapped her hands and held them to her breastbone. "It was made for you, Anna."

Anna turned around in front of the full-length mirror and looked over her shoulder to see how the dress looked from the back. It did fit her well. She imagined wearing the dress while out on a date with Mike and had to hold back a frown. She liked the thought of dating Mike, but what about Chandra? She loved her friend to death, but Chandra was staunchly loyal to Chad.

Devora cocked her head to the side. "What's wrong?"

"Nothing." Anna gave a bright smile. "I'll take the dress. Got any new shoes that would go with this dress?"

"Right this way." Devora gestured for Anna to follow her.

Anna padded across the carpeted floor as she followed Devora to the boutique's shoe section. "Those are adorable." Anna went straight to a pair of black heels with a single strap in front that went up the top of the foot to an ankle strap. The straps sparkled with crystals. "Freaking awesome."

Devora laughed. "I thought of you when they came in."

"You know me so well it's scary." Anna picked up one of the heels. "I'm guessing you have them in my size?"

"One pair, just for you." Devora gave a nod toward the back room. "I'll get them now and you can try them on."

If they fit, Anna knew she'd be going home with at least a stunning new dress and killer pair of heels. Of course she'd have to check out jewelry, too.

I'm a junkie, she thought as she held up the shoe. *Gotta have my fix.*

Devora returned, carrying a bright pink box, and Anna sat on the nearby padded bench and slipped on the heels. She walked around in them, trying them out, and looking at them in the full-length mirror. The shoes fit perfectly and looked just as good with the dress as Anna had thought they would.

She still had time to kill so she tried on more dresses and more shoes. She ended up with the first dress and shoes, a pair of black slacks, and a black sweater with a silky black camisole. She tended to where a lot of black. She also found jewelry to go along with each outfit she'd purchased.

Over an hour after entering the store, Anna carried her purchases to the door. With a look over her shoulder, Anna said, "See you, Devora."

Devora gave a wave. "Oh, I'd say within a week."

"Yes, you know me far too well." Anna looked at her packages and gave a rueful shake of her head. "See you then."

Devora grinned and the bells at the top of the door jangled as Anna let herself out into the night.

READ MORE OF *BELONG TO YOU HERE!*

ALSO BY CHEYENNE MCCRAY

~

(in reading order)

~Contemporary Cowboys~

Fencing You In

Tying You Down

Playing With You

Crazy For You

Hot For You

Made For You

Held By You

Belong To You

"Rough and Ready" Series
The Camerons

Silk and Spurs

Lace and Lassos

Champagne and Chaps

Satin and Saddles

Roses and Rodeo (with Creed McBride)

Lingerie and Lariats

Lipstick and Leather

"Armed and Dangerous" Series

Zack

Luke

Clay

Kade

Alex (a novella)

Eric (a novella)

~Romantic Suspense~

"Deadly Intent" Series

Hidden Prey

No Mercy

Taking Fire

Point Blank

"Recovery Enforcement Division" Series

Ruthless

Fractured

Vendetta

Single Title

Chosen Prey

Save by purchasing Boxed Sets

Riding Tall the First Boxed Set

Includes

Branded for You

Roping Your Heart

Fencing You In

Riding Tall the Second Boxed Set

Includes

Tying You Down

Playing with You

Crazy for You

Riding Tall the Third Boxed Set

Includes

Hot for You

Made for You

No Mercy

Taking Fire

Point Blank

~Paranormal Romance~

"Dark Sorcery" Series

The Forbidden

The Seduced

The Wicked

One Breath (novella)

The Shadows

The Dark

Cheyenne Writing as Debbie Ries

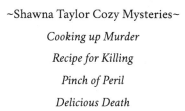

~Shawna Taylor Cozy Mysteries~

Cooking up Murder

Recipe for Killing

Pinch of Peril

Delicious Death

Taste of Danger

ABOUT CHEYENNE

Cheyenne McCray is an award-winning, *New York Times* and *USA Today* best-selling author who grew up on a ranch in southeastern Arizona and has written over one hundred published novels and novellas. Chey also writes cozy mysteries as **Debbie Ries**. She delights in creating stories of suspense, love, and redemption with characters and worlds her readers can get lost in.

Chey and her husband live with their two dogs in southeastern Arizona where she enjoys going on long walks, traveling around the world, and searching for her next adventure and new ideas, as well as hand embroidering crazy quilts and listening to audiobooks.

Find out more about Chey, how to contact her, and her books at **https://cheyennemccray.com.**

~

Sign up for Cheyenne's Newsletter
to keep up with Chey and her latest novels
http://cheyennemccray.com/newsletter

Made in the USA
Columbia, SC
02 January 2023

75450160R00124